What Was He Doing?

Seth drew back from Catty, his brain finally kicking in. This was the woman who could ruin his life— what little was left of it! Had he gone crazy?

He released her. Catty opened her eyes and blinked.

"I'm sorry," he said. "That was stupid."

Catty cleared her throat but couldn't manage any words. She looked positively stunned.

Seth stood up. "I don't know what got into me," he said.

In a split second he imagined what could have happened next. He would have taken her to bed, and spent the night making love to her, and the next morning he would have spilled every word of the family story. She'd take the next available transportation to New York and alert every branch of the armed forces stationed in the continental United States.

And he'd be a dead man in twenty-four hours!

Dear Reader:

As you can see, Silhouette Desire has a bold new cover design that we're all excited about. But while the overall look is new, two things remain the same. First, we've kept our eye-catching red border. You can be sure to always spot Silhouette Desires on the shelves! Second, between these new covers are the high-quality love stories that you've come to expect.

In addition, the MAN OF THE MONTH program continues with Mr. September, who comes from the pen of Dixie Browning. Clement Cornelius Barto is a unique hero who is sure to charm you with his unusual ways. But make no mistake, it's not just *Beginner's Luck* that makes him such a winner.

October brings you a man who's double the fun, because not only is Jody Branigan an exciting hero, he's also one of Leslie Davis Guccione's Branigan brothers. Look for his story in *Branigan's Touch*.

We at Silhouette have been happy to hear how much you've all enjoyed the Year of the Man. The responses we've received about the special covers— and to each and every one of our heroes—has been enthusiastic. Remember, there are more men ahead in 1989—don't let any of them get away!

Yours,

Lucia Macro
Senior Editor

NANCY MARTIN

A LIVING LEGEND

SILHOUETTE *Desire*

Published by Silhouette Books New York

America's Publisher of Contemporary Romance

SILHOUETTE BOOKS
300 East 42nd St., New York, N.Y. 10017

ISBN: 0-373-05522-6

First Silhouette Books printing September 1989

Books by Nancy Martin

Silhouette Intimate Moments

Black Diamonds #60

Silhouette Desire

Hit Man #461
A Living Legend #522

NANCY MARTIN

has lived in a succession of small towns in Pennsylvania, though she loves to travel to find locations for romance in larger cities in this country and abroad. Now she lives with her husband, their two daughters and an overly exuberant retriever in a house they've restored and are constantly tinkering with.

If Nancy's not sitting at her word processor with a stack of records on the stereo, you might find her cavorting with her children, skiing with her husband or relaxing by the pool. She loves writing romances and has also written as Elissa Curry.

One

Great," snapped the woman as she staggered to keep her balance in the wind that roared across Lake Superior. "Just terrific! How am I supposed to get off this godforsaken island if you won't wait for me?"

Waves smacked against the dock, spraying her sporty poplin jacket and brand-new hiking trousers. She clamped one hand over her wide-brimmed felt hat—the latest fall fashion in New York—and gripped her briefcase with her other. Black clouds boiled on the horizon, and the birch and pine trees hissed with a wind so strong it was blasting fallen leaves through the tumbled mass of her curly blond hair. The storm blowing down out of Canada was surely gale-force status.

The freckle-faced owner of the little boat that had brought her across the lake sat stubbornly in the stern of his craft, gripping the rudder for dear life. He raised his voice to be heard over the howl of the wind. "I ain't staying here all night, lady. Either you come back with me now or I'll fetch you in the morning when the weather's settled down!''

"I've got a job to do,'' she shouted at him. "And I never give up on a job. Don't you know who I am?''

"No, ma'am,'' yelled the boy, and he looked as if he was about to add something else—like maybe he didn't *care* to know who she was.

"I'm Catty Sinclair, you idiot.'' To prove her point, she let go of her hat and flashed a plastic-coated identification tag that she'd wrestled out of her jacket pocket. "I've been on *Good Morning America* four times! And right now I'm working on the biggest story of the century. *You're* missing your big chance to be a part of history!''

"Lady,'' he shouted, clearly unimpressed, "there's nothing worth reporting up here in these islands. Nobody in their right mind would live up here—not unless they're hiding from the FBI.''

"Exactly!''

He peered up at her through the first spattering of raindrops. "You sure don't look like the FBI, ma'am.''

"I'm *not* the FBI! I'm a reporter. A writer! Don't you people have television up here? Bookstores? Newspapers?'' Unable to keep her secret mission under wraps another instant, she burst out, "I'm here to find Rafer Fernando! You've heard of *him*, surely?''

The boy's eyes popped. "Rafer Fernando? The Prince of Rock and Roll? Lady, you're crazier than I thought. That guy's been dead for ten years!''

"That's what everybody *thinks*,'' Catty bellowed. "But I've got a lead that says he didn't die at all. He's been living *right here*, and I'm the one who's going to write his story!''

The boy shook his head. "You're nuts! Nobody lives up here!''

"Oh, no? What do you call *that*?''

Triumphantly, she pointed at the treetops where the outline of a steeply pitched roof was clearly visible. A map that had been carefully drawn by her source had brought Catty to exactly the right spot.

Her guide squinted up at the roof. "That?" he shouted. "That's just Mr. Bernstein. He's no rock-and-roll singer, lady, he's just as much of a loony as you are! Only *he's* dangerous! You better come back with me before he finds out you're here."

Catty lifted her briefcase and glared at the boy. "Don't try to intimidate me, kid. I don't threaten easily. *I* live in New York City!"

Her guide opened his mouth to argue some more, but quickly reconsidered and gave up. Without another word, he tipped his baseball cap, which proudly advertised Bob's Bait and Tackle, and then shoved off. He gunned the boat's little motor and began his long journey back the way they had come, leaving Catty Sinclair, world-renowned reporter who rarely left the canyons of Manhattan, standing on the deserted shores of a storm-blackened lake.

"You don't know what you're missing!" Catty shouted after him, unmindful that her words were snatched away by the wind. "Your name could be a headline on every supermarket tabloid in America!"

Catty watched the boat chug across the waves, and for an instant she felt a prickle of panic. Sure, she could come on like gangbusters, but inside she was quivering. She even raised her hand to call the boat back, intending to beg the kid to stay, maybe even bribe him. She'd never been abandoned in the wilderness, after all. But begging would be humiliating, and Catty had once vowed never to be humiliated again.

So she snatched her hand down and, after just a second's hesitation, whirled around and headed for the shore, struggling to hold on to her hat and rummage through her briefcase at the same time. "Ignorant hillbillies," she muttered to herself, angry for feeling weak even for a moment.

The dock was wet, and an iridescent film of gasoline was slippery underfoot. Catty skidded, nearly plunging into the lake, but caught her balance just in time by grabbing a pine tree branch. Gingerly, she staggered onto the rocky shore. Boulders slick with lichen were separated by patches of rank weeds. She spotted a break in the trees farther up—maybe a path. Muttering to herself, Catty began to climb over the rocks.

She grabbed for a handhold in the bushes and heaved herself upward. Her Italian-made boots slithered ineffectually on the stone, more proof that she should have made better plans before jumping into this story with such abandon. Panting as though she'd run the Boston Marathon, she discovered she'd traveled less than ten yards. Suddenly the bush she'd been hanging on to gave way and Catty slipped, landing on her backside with a squishy plop.

"Damn!" She'd landed in a puddle. The seat of her new trousers was totally soaked through. "What kind of godforsaken place *is* this?"

"It's *my* godforsaken place," growled a male voice above her on the trail. "Now who the hell are you?"

The first thing she noticed was that he was carrying a gun. A big gun.

Catty clambered to her feet, raised her hands over her head and tried her damnedest to manufacture a cocky grin. "Let me guess," she said as ingenuously as possible. "This is your island and your name is Gilligan and you live here with a bunch of castaways, right?"

He did not smile back at her.

He was a tall man with a whip-thin body encased in jeans and a big-shouldered mountain parka. His face was hard and sharp-featured with at least three days' worth of beard that made guessing his age difficult. His hair was black, long and shaggy, as though it were growing out from a month-old haircut. Catty had a quick impression of flecks of gray at his temples.

But most arresting were his eyes—black and burning with such hostility that Catty took an involuntary step backward.

The weapon resting alertly in his hands was of the shotgun variety, and from the way he handled it, it looked dangerous, indeed. Jeremiah Johnson meets Rambo, Catty thought.

She swallowed hard and tried to muster a friendly smile. "Look," she said, "I wonder if you would mind putting that thing down? It's quite distracting and makes me a little nervous, you see, and I want to be absolutely clearheaded when I explain to you who I am."

He narrowed his eyes and made a quick inspection of her figure, as if expecting her to pull a missile launcher out of her briefcase or a machete from her hip pocket. There was more than mere suspicion in his expression, though. He was ready for serious trouble.

She raised her hands higher and wiggled her fingers. "I'm harmless. See?"

Still visibly wary, he lowered the muzzle. He hadn't exactly been pointing it at her, Catty told herself, but when he finally crooked the gun under his arm, she relaxed.

"Well, isn't this much nicer? How do you do?" She cheerfully marched up the trail toward him, her hand extended for a friendly shake. "My name is Catty Sinclair. What's yours?"

He ignored her hand. "What are you doing here?"

His voice was low, barely a rumble, which made Catty's sound loud and raucous even to her own ears. "Well, I'd like to explain that in detail to your employer. Perhaps you could take me to him?"

"My what?"

"The man you work for. Mr. Bernstein is his name, so I hear. You're some kind of caretaker, I assume?"

He did look like some kind of classic henchman—a daunting specimen with a tough-smoldering look and a pair of strong-looking hands that appeared capable of wringing necks.

Catty tried her winning smile again. "It would save a heck of a lot of time if I just talked to you both at the same time."

Stone-faced, he said, "This is private land. You'll have to leave."

"But I've come such a long way to talk to this Bernstein character!"

"I'm sorry the trip was for nothing. There isn't anybody else to speak to, miss. I'm alone here."

Catty managed to fake a flirty look. "Maybe I'll have a look around anyway, just to be sure."

He barred her path by moving the barrel of the shotgun. "There's no need," he said. "This island is deserted. You'll just get hurt."

"Oh, I'm tougher than I look."

He glanced at her again, clearly not believing her for a moment. Her jacket was stiff with newness, her trousers still creased. Her boots were totally wrong for the terrain, and the expensive leather briefcase she'd dropped on the trail looked more suitable for a *Fortune* 500 boardroom than the back of beyond.

He shook his head. "It's out of the question. You'll have to leave."

"I *can't* leave," she said patiently. "My transportation just disappeared. See? That's him out there on the lake. I'm stuck here, so you might as well—"

"You didn't ask him to stay?"

"Of course I did, but he chickened out. I couldn't very well clobber him with my tape recorder and hijack his boat, could I?"

"Why didn't you bring your own?"

"My own *boat*? Heavens, I don't even drive a car!"

At that, he looked disgusted as well as suspicious. "What did you say your name was?"

"Catty. Catty Sinclair. What's *yours*, while we're on the subject?"

He looked at her, obviously believing she was a Soviet spy. "You don't need to know," he said.

Remarks of that nature just made Catty more curious than ever. If she'd been a real cat, she was sure her whiskers would be twitching. She could smell an interesting story a mile away, and she'd written a string of highly successful unauthorized biographical articles to prove it. Catty Sinclair was a name that set newspaper publishers to salivating. She had a nose for scandalous tales, and one look at this gun-toting Heathcliff told her there was a hell of a story in the wind.

"Maybe I've made a mistake," she said. "Are *you* Bernstein?"

"It doesn't matter who I am," he said. "You're leaving."

"For crying out *loud*!" she declared. "Whether you like it or not, I'm stranded here for the night! It's raining! What kind of man are you? There's a typhoon on its way, I'm slowly *freezing* to death, and you're playing the guy who guards the gates of hell! There's obviously a perfectly cozy house up there in the trees, so why don't we make the best of a bad situation and go inside? You're stuck with me! I'm sorry, but that's the way it goes. Am I getting through to you, handsome?"

He stared at her, clearly amazed to find a blond, briefcase-toting harridan with a New Jersey accent yelling in the middle of his island paradise. Whether her arguments penetrated, Catty couldn't tell. His face remained cold and revealed nothing. Catty held her breath.

"Cerberus," he said at last. "He was a dog, not a man."

"What?"

"The dog who guards the gate of hell."

He turned on his heel then. With the shotgun tucked under his arm, he led the way up the trail into the shelter of the pine trees. The wind whistled down from the sky at that moment, bringing the first onslaught of hailstones. The weather didn't seem to faze Heathcliff, though. He hiked upward several paces, then looked back. "Come along," he said.

Catty needed no further invitation. She scrambled after him, one thought shining like a beacon in her mind. The whole story might even make one hell of a terrific book.

The building nestled in the trees was not exactly the palatial hideaway of a reclusive rock-and-roll star. Catty felt a pang of disappointment when she finally got a clear look at it. The house was little more than a log cabin with a veranda out front and a small shanty in the back that could be nothing else but an outdoor latrine. A curl of smoke eddied from the chimney. Otherwise, there was nothing to see but trees, a woodpile and an upside-down canoe propped against the house.

Under the wind-whipped trees it was nearly dark, so Catty stumbled up the stone steps to stay close to her guide. Her footsteps on the wooden porch caused an immediate uproar of barking from inside the cabin.

"Stay here," Heathcliff ordered when they had gained the porch. "The dogs won't bite if you hold still."

He went inside the cabin, and to make sure Catty didn't budge, he allowed two dogs to come barreling out.

Then her host disappeared inside. The dogs flung themselves at her, barking, panting and slobbering.

"Nice doggies," Catty said in a very small voice.

The dogs looked ferocious, leaping around her on powerful, springlike legs. It took almost two full minutes before she realized they were wagging their tails and showing every sign of being delighted to have company. They weren't slavering mastiffs, either, just a couple of frisky Labrador retrievers. Catty risked her life by moving one foot and then the other. Neither of the dogs bit her. One of them shoved his wet snout into her hand, and she patted his head nervously.

Then she bolted into the cabin and slammed the screen behind her. The rejected dogs whined and scratched the door.

The inside of the cabin was more interesting than the outside. The furniture was mostly old, comfortable-looking pine pieces with some overstuffed chintz pillows so faded they probably dated from the fifties. Catty noted a cheery fire crackling in the limestone hearth. An earthenware bowl full of apples sat on the varnished trestle table, and there was an old gas stove with an antique icebox beside it. A selection of copper-bottomed pots and iron skillets hung from a rack on the ceiling. A large array of fishing rods was lined up along the wall by the back door, and the unmistakable odor of fish wafted in the otherwise woodsy-smelling air. And everywhere—all over the walls, under the windows and tucked beneath the stairs—were bookshelves lined with volumes of every size and shape. The place was practically a public library.

Catty's gaze ran back to the center of the room where a flight of rough-sawn wooden steps rose to the second floor, nothing more than a loft, really, complete with exposed rafters. She could see a mound of quilts piled on a big pine-framed bed, and a couple of faded flannel shirts were draped over the railing. No skylights, no potted ferns around the Jacuzzi. No *Lifestyles of the Rich and Famous.*

Catty nearly choked on her disappointment. First of all, the place was clearly the home of one man, not two. And it hardly looked like the kind of place a millionaire rock-and-roll legend would call home—even if he *had* dropped out of society. There was no suggestion of luxury. No gold records hung on the walls. There were books everywhere, not guitars. It looked more like the home of an absentminded professor turned monk.

Catty leaned over the nearest rocking chair and picked up the book that had been left on the cushion. *Tah's Principles of Meditation in Yoga.* Catty dropped it as though she'd been burned.

She directed her attention to her host and studied him with laserlike intensity. Was *this* Rafer Fernando? If so, he'd changed his appearance significantly. Of course Catty hadn't expected to find him in his trademark black T-shirt and silver-buckled belt, drinking Jack Daniels and holding a buxom groupie in each arm, but this was ridiculous! Yoga and flannel shirts? Meditation instead of cocaine?

He was digging through a drawer in the kitchen, his back turned to her. Without looking, he reached out a hand and flipped a switch on a large radiotelephone on the counter. He'd propped the shotgun against the stove near his leg.

The dogs whined louder at the screen door, causing her host to turn and see Catty. He frowned. "I thought I told you to stay outside."

"The dogs invited me in," Catty cracked, hoping she sounded tough. She made a hasty beeline for the fireplace and stood there, rubbing her hands together. "I was cold. Don't worry. I'm not a kleptomaniac."

He shot her a glare and began to tinker with the radio. "Well, just stay where you are," he ordered. "I don't want you wandering all over the place."

She didn't move, but let her gaze roam freely. She spotted a group of photographs on one wall and wished she could stroll over for a closer look. Some were sepia in tone, others were simply black and white. They appeared to be family groups, some with fish as their focal points.

Then she looked at her host again. Handsome as hell under the mountain man getup. In the city he'd probably have women swooning at his feet—women who were accustomed to the guys in three-piece suits, guys who exercised in sparkling clean gyms with fancy weight equipment and drank bottled water to stay healthy. He was a little rough around the edges—his hair definitely needed to be cut, and his clothes looked as if they'd been hanging on pegs for a decade or so. But when he stripped off his parka, Catty saw that his body was splendid. Nice long legs, shoulders that could make a grown woman howl at the moon. And his lithe way of moving was hard not to watch. He had muscle where most men were very boring. If he was Rafer, he'd shaped up.

Unaware of her attention, he fiddled with the radio and finally began to speak, trying to make contact with someone he called Kozak. No one responded to his hail until several minutes had passed, during which time her host became more and more annoyed. Then a gruff male voice finally answered. Catty could barely make out the conversation for all the static.

"That you, Bernstein?" a voice called at last.

"Yeah, Kozak," he responded, glancing grimly at Catty once his pseudonym was out in the open. To his radio contact, he said, "I've got a problem."

"Go ahead, old buddy."

"An uninvited guest dropped in. A woman who hired a boat from Deer Lick, but they left without her. You have anybody who can come pick her up?"

The response Catty heard was laughter.

Impatiently, her host snapped, "Come on, Kozak, I don't need this aggravation."

The laughter continued. Then, "You could use that kind of aggravation for a night or two, Bernstein. Just tuck her in and keep her warm, then bring her over yourself when the weather clears. Or keep her till spring, if she's willing. Your choice."

"Give me a break, Mike. I can't have her here!"

"Nothing I can do, Bernstein. Storm looks bad. I'm not risking one of my boats to save you from a sex-starved female. Just hang tough, old buddy."

The man by the name of Bernstein came close to punching the radio. But he restrained himself and instead slammed down the receiver and nearly tore the switch off when he shut down the equipment. He cursed his bad luck, then cursed again.

Then he transferred his glare to the woman. She looked like the kind of urban female he'd only read about—with a mop of curly blond hair sticking out from a goofy-looking hat, a body like a slightly voluptuous elf and a face like Barbra Streisand's. She had a long busybody's nose, a full, tilting mouth, brown Cleopatra eyes that sparkled with greedy curiosity.

Her clothes were just on the edge of outrageousness. She'd made an attempt to look outdoorsy with the safari jacket and pants, but he could see the gleam of gold jewelry in her earlobes and around her neck, and a flashy scarf was tucked with Isadora Duncan panache around her neck.

And she moved constantly, too. Her glittering gaze zipped from one spot to another as if she wanted to memorize every detail of her surroundings—probably so she could make a report at her next society cocktail party. Her hands reached to touch things—his books, the stones of the fireplace, the pillows on the furniture. She seemed to need to learn their textures, feel their weight, before moving on to the next item of interest. A seismograph could have registered the energy vibrating from inside her. She even tapped her boots on the floor. What for? he wondered. Did she expect to find a trapdoor beneath her feet?

He felt invaded, almost panicky. He knew he had to figure a way to get rid of her. Quickly.

She began to stroll, endeavoring to look innocent, but instead looking more and more suspicious with every step. She said, "So you're Mr. Bernstein! I have a friend who married a Bernstein a couple of years ago. In Hoboken. You have any relatives in Hoboken by any chance?"

"No."

She smiled sweetly, taking no heed of his terse tone. "I guess you don't sound like an East Coast type. Where are you from?"

"Here."

She smiled some more. He supposed it was meant to be a winsome smile, but it just looked calculating to him. "Oh, of course," she said. "Silly of me." She picked up the book he'd been reading and put it down again before cruising toward the shelves. "You must have a lot of spare time up here in fisherman's paradise."

He didn't answer.

"For reading, I mean," she went on. "Are these all your books? It's quite a collection." She began to pull one volume after another down off the shelves, leafing through them aimlessly, chattering the whole time. "Your tastes are pretty mixed, too. *Comparative Eastern Religions.* That's never been my bag. Look at this—biology, chemistry. What are you, some kind of scientist? And poetry, too. Hey, this one's inscribed. See? 'For Seth.' Is that you? 'Happy birthday, Mom.' Gee, that's sweet. So your first name is Seth." She turned and smiled, a moppet with a hard gleam in her eye.

He crossed the room in four strides and snatched the book from her hands.

She dropped the fake innocence. "Hey!"

"Look, Miss Sinclair, I don't know what you're up to—"

"I'm just being friendly."

"Bull. You didn't come sneaking in here just to chat about books."

She didn't flinch, and suddenly he realized she'd baited him into coming closer. He felt the warmth of her body, the heat of her curiosity. She stood very still and squinted at him, taking a good, long look at his face.

Abruptly, she said, "Have you had plastic surgery?"

"What?"

"Do you wear contact lenses?"

He stared at her. "Are you crazy?"

"Are you Rafer Fernando?"

"*What?*"

"Answer the question. Are you or are you not Rafer Fernando?"

The suggestion was so bizarre that he figured he'd heard wrong. But he replayed the words in his head and they came out the same. He stepped back and said, "I hope you brought your own straightjacket. You're a lunatic!"

"Come on, you can tell me the truth." She followed him around the furniture until he reached the kitchen and quickly put the counter between them. He had to get away from her, but she put her hands flat on the counter and leaned toward him. "I'm a professional," she coaxed. "You can trust me. Together we can astound the world!"

"You can astound the world all by yourself," he retorted. "You don't need me!"

"Of course I do! The Rafer Fernando story will be the biggest story to hit the press since Pearl Harbor! I need details. I know all the right people, and we can orchestrate it perfectly, but you have to—"

"Hold it," he commanded. "You came up here because you think I'm some kind of singer? You think I'm— Wait a minute. I thought that Fernando guy was dead."

"But you're not, are you? You faked a suicide and you've been living here in isolation for— Those *are* contact lenses, aren't they? Fernando had blue eyes. And you seem taller." She frowned. "Are you wearing lifts or something? Come on, tell me everything!" She wrestled a notepad out of her pocket.

Seth reached across the counter and grabbed her wrist. The notepad cluttered out of her hand. "I want some answers, too."

She resisted, and when she saw the look on his face, she pulled back instinctively, consternation puckering her brow.

He gripped her wrist harder and felt her pulse jump. Her eyes were brown, the color of chestnuts, her skin soft—undeniably female. Her perfume, a strong scent in the cabin, conjured up memories he thought he'd banished for years. He tried to tamp them down once more and concentrate on the trouble at hand. "Where did you hear about me?" he asked.

She thrust out her jaw. "I've got my sources. I'm a journalist."

He snorted. "Journalist! Anyone who can string a few sentences together thinks they've found an easy way to make a buck. Tell me the truth. How did you know I was here?"

"Ouch! You're hurting me!"

"I could do worse," he said from between clenched teeth.

"I don't have to reveal a source. The First Amendment—"

"The First Amendment says you're allowed to scream before I strangle you, too. Except nobody out here is going to hear a single squeak. Tell me, damn you!"

"From a guy," she said, gasping. "A man who lives in Deer Lick."

He grabbed the shoulder of her jacket with his other hand, adrenaline seething in his veins. "What guy? Who was it?"

She gulped, truly scared and staring. "He owns a newspaper there—strictly small potatoes. He called a paper in New York a couple of days ago with the scoop. They don't send their reporters on stuff like this, so they hired me—free-lance work, you know? They pay my expenses and I get the rights to a book—"

"I don't give a damn about you," he snapped. "Who else knows I'm here?"

"How should *I* know? I just—"

"The paper in New York. The editors?"

"What's your *problem*?"

"Talk, blast you!"

She did, crying out when he twisted her arm. "The editors thought you might be Rafer Fernando, that's all. There's no real proof. The man in Deer Lick told me about a recluse named Bernstein, so I came. Cripes, will you let me go?"

"Shut up. Are you going to bring boatloads of sightseers up here?"

"You're a big story!"

"Damn you—"

"But you're *my* big story for the moment," she added swiftly. "I've made sure I have an exclusive on this."

"What does that mean?"

"There won't be any sightseers. Not for a while. Not yet, at least. You can trust me, Rafer."

He released her jacket. Shaking his head, he tried to calm himself, to get a grip on his composure. She stared up at him, and he felt his gut tighten at the sight of her excitement, her desire.

Curtly, he said, "I'm not Rafer Fernando."

Her face changed, showing profound dismay. She believed him. For a second she looked like a kid who didn't get the red bike for Christmas. It was almost comical.

But it didn't last long. She sucked in a hissing breath and didn't move. But as she looked up at him, narrowing her eyes, something else crept into Catty Sinclair's expression. Curiosity dawned. Whatever story she had planned was replaced by a new idea. Softly, she said, "Then who are you?"

He gave her a shove and stood back. "I'm nobody," he said, suddenly appalled by his own behavior. Manhandling women was just one more thing he could add to his list of new pastimes. He'd let the frustration get out of hand. The first woman who'd entered his domain in four years of exile had chased caution out of his head completely. A wave of self-disgust rose within him.

Turning away from her, he said, "Take my advice, Miss Sinclair. Go home and forget you ever heard about me."

She rubbed her wrist and watched him. "Why?"

He said—too softly for her to hear, he was sure, "Because I don't exist anymore."

Two

One good journalistic quality Catty knew she had going for herself was her adaptability. If a story didn't feel like it was going to pan out, she dropped it and moved on.

Her gut feeling was that Seth Bernstein—if that was his real name—was not the legendary rock-and-roll singer she'd been searching for. She massaged her wrist where he'd gripped her and knew he'd done so with a strength born of desperation. Catty knew desperation when she saw it, and Mr. Bernstein had a lot of it.

If he wasn't Rafer Fernando, who *was* he? She felt like a foxhound with a snootful of a wonderful scent, a shark tasting fresh blood, a fine racehorse boxed in at the starting gate. A dangerous but attractive recluse hiding under an assumed name was a tantalizing idea, always a winner with publishers. And this one had secrets he was very worried about revealing. Plus he looked like a photographer's dream—all that wild hair, the lanky, balanced body and those burning black eyes. Had she stumbled onto an even better story?

"Well, look," she said cheerily, determined not to scare him off before she learned more, "I'm sorry about the mix-up. If you're not Rafer, I guess I'll just apologize for the intrusion and clear out of here. I'm just sorry I can't leave before morning."

He looked at her suspiciously, clearly not sure whether he should trust this change in tactics. Without responding, he picked up the shotgun, crossed the room to a gun rack over the fireplace mantel and put the weapon away.

"You're pretty quick with that gun, aren't you?" Catty said, grinning. "What were you expecting? Some kind of invasion?"

"Some kids broke into this place last spring," he said shortly. "I was gone at the time, and they did some damage. I don't want them thinking this is their party hangout."

"I see. Well, that's logical. You can't have people interrupting you all the time. You must have work to do."

When he didn't respond, she smiled and blinked innocently. "What kind of work *do* you do up here all alone?"

"I fish," he said.

"Commercially?"

"No, for myself."

"I see. Anything else?"

"No."

She felt sure he was lying, but let the answer stand. "Well, you certainly have a truck load of books in this place, Bernstein. You must read by the hour!"

"Most of these books have been here for years. Long before I came."

"So it's not really your cabin?"

He obviously wished he could terminate the cross-examination, but he knew he couldn't do it without arousing her curiosity even further. Slowly, he said, "It belongs to my family. I'm just using it for a while."

"Your family must love the outdoors," she enthused, starting to stroll away from him. She unpeeled the scarf from around her neck, preparing to make herself at home. "Just look at these photos! I've never seen fish so big! Is that man your father or something? He's got your look—pensive, but don't-mess-around-with-me. And this high jumper—why, that's you, isn't it? Nice legs. You ever consider modeling? I've got some good contacts—"

He caught her elbow and smoothly steered Catty away from the display of framed family photographs. "Those are mostly distant relatives. People who vacationed up here decades ago." Then he switched tactics, too, suddenly making an effort to appear friendly. "Listen, are you hungry? I was going to fix some supper."

"Great! I'm starved. I had a hamburger in Deer Lick, but that was hours ago."

"Fine. I'm not accustomed to having guests, though," said Bernstein, releasing her arm as easily as he'd seized it. "Would you mind lending a hand?"

Catty saw through the ruse at once. He intended to keep her busy and far away from any clues that might explain who he was and what he was doing. Well, he couldn't keep her busy until morning!

She hoped she sounded utterly guileless. "Sure! Any guest who drops in the way I did should certainly have to sing for her supper. What can I do?"

He led her to the kitchen. Catty took off her jacket and rolled up the sleeves of her pink sweater. He put her to work peeling the last two potatoes in his bin, but it took Catty a few minutes to remove all her rings and bracelets before she could actually get down to peeling. She planned her attack while he assembled an iron skillet, a yellow onion and some oil. She needed to figure a way to get him out of the cabin so she could sweep the place for clues.

He reached a long arm past her to snap some leaves off the plants that were lined up along the window sill.

"Wolfsbane?" Catty asked lightly. "Nightshade? I know I invited myself rather rudely, Bernstein, but I already apologized—"

"Don't worry," he said, not cracking a smile. "These are ordinary herbs. Nothing poisonous. Will you do me a favor?"

"Name it."

"Call me Seth."

"Oh. Sure."

He lifted two fish out of the icebox—fish with heads and eyes and tails and everything.

Catty gulped and averted her gaze. Hoping to keep her mind off the unfamiliar ingredients he was mixing for her consumption, she began to peel potatoes with a vengeance. "Tell me about yourself," she encouraged.

"Nothing much to tell," he said, busy with a knife of his own. "I don't get off the island often. You're a reporter, I assume? Where do you work?"

He was hardly subtle about turning the tables on her, and even though Catty knew he was putting her off, she soon found herself chattering to keep her mind off the fish eyes. She told him about her book contract with Peacock Publishing and the free-lance work she was doing for magazines and tabloids to make ends meet until she found the right subject for her next book. She talked a lot, in fact. He was a good listener. Or perhaps a sly one. Silently, he went about preparing the meal, even taking the half-peeled potato from Catty's hands and finishing the job himself when she really got to talking.

In fact, he had food on the table in a very short time, and Catty realized she hadn't really done much to help. He had simply gone about fixing the meal while encouraging her to chatter about subjects he couldn't possibly care about. Long ago Catty had perfected the art of telling amusing anecdotes about the celebrities she often interviewed in order to deflect interest in herself. It was always easier to talk about famous people than Catty Sinclair.

As he carried their plates to the trestle table, she described for him the night she found a well-known, ponytailed television actress misbehaving in a nightclub and the details of the star's subsequent arrest, including how she whacked the police officer over the head with her alligator purse.

"So I told the nightclub manager," Catty said, "that I'd pay him fifty bucks anytime he had another scoop for me, and it's been a great investment. That club is one of the best places to find celebrities with their hair down."

"But don't you feel uncomfortable," Seth said at last, "printing gossip about people who believe you're their friend?"

"It's not gossip. It's fact. It happened, and I was there. Look, I print information about people who have chosen to sell their images to the public. Most of that talk about privacy is for show. Why, famous people even hawk baby pictures of their own kids to magazines all the time! I'm just helping them reach the public eye."

"Any publicity is good publicity as long as you spell the names right, is that it?"

"That's the name of the game."

"Hmm," said Seth, looking unconvinced.

"I'm only doing what they want me to do," Catty insisted. "It's perfectly legal."

He looked her in the eye for the first time all evening. "But is it right?"

Catty looked squarely back at him, lifting her chin. "It's a living," she said.

"Hmm," Seth murmured again, not a judgmental syllable, just an acknowledging one. The subject slid away. With steady hands, he used a match to light the oil lamp on the table, and when the warm glow of the flame grew around them, Catty realized how thoroughly darkness had fallen outside. Rain rattled on the windows and made a muffled drone on the roof. Seth studied the table, making sure he had taken care of everything. Then he asked, "Would you like a glass of wine?"

"Yeah, sounds great."

While he went to get the bottle, Catty sat down in one of the chairs. She examined her plate. The fish had been fried in cornmeal and herbs and now looked like something edible—crisply golden with a curl of fragrant steam that rose to tease her nose. The potato had been quartered and sautéed to perfection along with slices of vegetable, which he'd arranged around the edges of the plate. The effect was simple, but colorful and definitely appetizing.

Oddly enough, however, it made Catty nervous. Having dinner one-on-one with a man wasn't an everyday occurrence for her—she was more the type who grabbed a deli sandwich and ate meals at her desk. And Bernstein had a dangerous quality so many women found attractive but Catty found just plain unsettling.

As usual, her reaction to nervousness was to talk.

"I had a dinner that looked just like this in Paris once," Catty called to him from her seat. "It was terrific, let me tell you. Just wonderful! The French publisher paid for the whole works—tips for the doorman and everything. I even got reimbursed for the plane ticket!"

Seth returned to the table with a bottle of wine in one hand and two ordinary drinking glasses in the other. "How was the food?"

"What?"

"Did you enjoy the meal?"

"Of course! We cut a deal on a story that ran in eight newspapers all over Europe. I made almost twenty thousand dollars in the end."

Sounding somewhat dry, he said, "Congratulations."

He uncorked the bottle and poured Catty's glass first, then his own. That done, he folded his lanky frame into the chair across from hers. Everything he did was slow and deliberate, as if he intended to enjoy the food all the more because of the ceremony of preparation. He didn't put his hands together, bow his head and recite a childhood prayer, but he took a moment and seemed to relax, or perhaps stretch out all his senses.

Without thinking, Catty said suddenly, "You probably think I'm pretty bizarre."

"Unusual," he corrected, meeting her eyes unwillingly.

"I suppose you don't get many journalists up this way too often?"

He picked up his fork and began to eat. "No journalists," he said after he'd swallowed the first bite of fish. "An occasional Boy Scout in the summer, but that's about all the traffic I see."

Catty dug in, too. "Your friend Kozak, though. That's somebody you see now and then, right?"

Seth nodded. "He owns a store across the lake."

"In Deer Lick?"

"No, there's no town where Kozak is." After a moment during which he obviously decided what information could be safely divulged, he said, "It's a kind of supply station a few miles from here, that's all. People like me buy fuel, food, that sort of thing. That way we don't have to do business in Deer Lick."

"Why do you say that? You don't like Deer Lick?"

He continued to eat his meal, saying briefly, "Too many people."

Mulling that over, Catty ate also. The fish—which she had not been prepared to enjoy—was excellent. She paid her compliments to the chef, and chattered a bit too long about a Beverly Hills cook she'd interviewed once to learn all the dietary eccentricities of a handsome movie idol with a penchant for raw meat and aphrodisiacs. Seth listened to the story while he ate but didn't comment. After a while, Catty began to feel as if she was telling racy jokes to a priest.

She concentrated on wolfing down her meal. The delicate herbal flavors of the food were enhanced by the wine, a dry white with a natural effervescence. The label was in French. Catty drank half a glassful and expressed her surprise at the quality of the vintage.

"This is very good vino, if you ask me." She raised her glass as if to salute the wine. "Is your pal Kozak a wine connoisseur, too?"

Seth shook his head. "Kozak doesn't drink anything but water, as far as I know."

"Good Lord!" Catty laughed. "You people really believe in clean living, don't you?"

Seth polished off his meal before he answered. Then he pushed his plate an inch and said, "Mike Kozak is an alcoholic. He had a problem, and he needed a way to solve it. That's why he lives here."

Catty felt a stab of discomfort. She'd said the wrong thing and made a jerk of herself. Alcoholism was something she'd seen firsthand, and she'd put that time far behind, along with a few other memories. But she made no apologies for her remark. That wasn't her style. She simply leaned closer to him and asked, "Why do *you* live here?"

He picked up his wine. Resting both elbows on the table, Seth looked at her over the rim of the glass. For a moment, Catty thought she imagined that he might have smiled. His black eyes seemed more full of light suddenly.

He said, "I can see why you're such a successful reporter. I've never met anyone as persistent as you are."

Catty grinned. "It's one of my best qualities, don't you think?"

"It can be," he said carefully, "a little exasperating."

She laughed. "I can't help it. It's instinctive. Even when I was a kid, I was the nosiest brat in the projects. I knew what was going on in every apartment."

"You grew up in the city?"

"Yeah. Atlantic City, New Jersey. In an underprivileged neighborhood—that's what they're called now."

"What did you call it?"

"A slum," said Catty matter-of-factly. "But I don't live there anymore, and that's what's important. I learned one important lesson there—that if you don't count your change, you deserve to be ripped off. I've come a hell of a long way on that motto."

"Sounds like an interesting story."

Catty snorted. "Interesting? No way. You won't catch *me* looking back. I learned years ago that the only interesting stories anyone wants to hear are about rich and famous people, nothing about broken homes or fathers who beat their—well, that's why I chose my particular line of work. I know how to make a profit. Give me a stupid starlet any day. Or a womanizing politician. *That's* interesting reading."

Seth watched her. "You make it sound like a threat."

"Do I?" Catty shook her head. "I don't steal anything from anybody. Let's get that straight. I don't suck up to famous people, get them to talk and then run like hell to the nearest newspaper office with their life's secrets. Maybe I have a few scruples about using people. I only write about names in the public domain—people who are looking for publicity. Politicians on the make, Hollywood gold diggers. I don't make friends with my subjects. I just do my job."

"That must make for a lonely life."

Catty eyed him. "You care to make a comment about loneliness, Mr. Seth Bernstein? The man who doesn't exist anymore? You didn't think I heard that, did you?"

He stood up and began to clear away the dishes. It took a full minute for Catty to realize he didn't intend to answer the question at all.

That was new to her. She wasn't used to people ignoring what she asked. But he had simply walked away. And something in his demeanor—Catty wasn't sure what exactly—stopped her from demanding a response. He had an almost Zenlike calm about him, so different from the flaring temper he'd displayed when he grabbed her earlier. Which was the real man?

He cut up an apple and proceeded to eat the slices for dessert as he washed the dishes. He pumped water into the aluminum sink with the hand pump, then washed each plate and piece of silver and rinsed them with water he boiled in a kettle on the gas stove. He used the same hot water to make a cup of instant coffee for himself and one for Catty, and he drank his black while scrubbing the skillet. Without being asked, Catty dried the dishes with a frayed linen towel. His silence made her uncomfortable. Was he angry? Or just ignoring her?

After the dishes were put away, Seth let the dogs in from the porch and fed them from a bin of dry dog food.

"Well, now what?" Catty asked when the room had been put back in order.

"Bed," said Seth.

He felt like laughing when he said the word. Suddenly the cocksure girl from the big city looked as if he'd suggested something illegal. She even backed up three paces until she collided with the nearest chair.

"B-bed?" she repeated.

"I get up early," he explained. "It's a waste of kerosene to stay up long past sundown. Besides, the fish stop biting as soon as the sun hits the water, so if I want to eat, I've got to get out on the lake before sunrise."

She tried to wipe the look of anxiety off her face. "I see," she said, and gulped so that her throat made a funny noise. The subject of sex clearly had not occurred to her until that moment.

It had occurred to Seth, however. It had been a surprise, he had to admit, because Catty Sinclair wasn't exactly the kind of woman who haunted his dreams at night. She was cute in spite of the tough-talking image she projected, but she wasn't exactly going to set the world on fire with her brains or beauty. Still, she had a lovely mouth he couldn't seem to take his eyes off, and the soft pink sweater she wore both revealed and concealed a figure that affected Seth in ways he'd forgotten the human body could react. Her perfume filled his head. The memory of her silky skin against his hands remained vivid. Her shape, hidden amid the casually sloppy folds of her stylish clothes, intrigued him. She was slim, but not racing lean. Soft, but not plush.

And the sound of her laughter stirred Seth into feeling something close to delight. In spite of himself, he liked the way she tossed her head and set the flossy blond curls of her hair to dancing when she laughed. He enjoyed the sparkle in her face when she talked, the animation in her hands when she wanted answers. She had a streak of wickedness, a dash of spice.

But it was perhaps the flash of uncertainty that crossed her face from time to time that touched Seth most. The expression made him think of a little girl who didn't get enough attention at home, a homeless puppy who'd been kicked once too often. She was brave and gritty on the outside, but he thought he could see something softer beneath the prickly armor she wore.

"Listen," she said, apparently shaken by the sudden prospect of spending the night with him, "I'm a night owl, so you might as well run along and get a good night's rest. Go ahead. I'll just stay down here with Rover and Spot."

"Sam and Betsy."

"Right." Hastily, she went on, "I've got some notes to go through, anyway. For another piece I'm working on. Oh, but you don't want the light on, do you? Well, I—you go to sleep. An early night might be good for me, too."

"There's a perfectly comfortable bed upstairs—"

"It's yours," she said. "I'll catnap on the floor, honest. I've got a bad back, anyway. A strange bed practically puts me in traction."

He had a feeling she was lying, but decided not to press the point. "How about a blanket, at least?"

"Fine, great," she said quickly. "That'd be terrific."

"And a towel for washing up. You'll want to scrub that goop off your face before you—"

"Goop? This is Elizabeth Arden's finest, buster!"

Her brows came down in a gloriously angry frown, which assured Seth that he'd coaxed her out of her worried state.

He suppressed a smile. "Anything else you need?"

She shook her head stiffly. "I always pack supplies for an emergency. Toothbrush and whatnot. I'll be fine. Good night."

So Seth pointed out the path to the bathroom facilities, left her alone and went to bed. Sleep wasn't long in coming, but he had a strange dream as the storm passed—a dream that wasn't entirely unpleasant.

Catty's night was infinitely less enjoyable.

First of all, she *hated* sleeping on the floor. The blanket wasn't warm enough, but she was afraid to sleep too near the fire for fear an errant spark might fly out and set her ablaze. The floor was horribly uncomfortable, but what was worse was the two dogs. Sam and Betsy wouldn't leave her alone. It seemed they liked having her to sleep with. They curled up on either side of Catty and took turns licking her face throughout the night.

"Go away, you flea-bitten morons! Go lick *him*, will you?"

She clutched her blanket and tried not to imagine that she might soon be joined by another sleeping partner. Only Seth Bernstein might want to do more than lick her face. Maybe he was a crazed sex maniac hiding from justice! An ax murderer? Catty lay stiff as a plank, listening for the sound of stealthy footsteps creeping up on her. She tried very hard to keep a lid on her active imagination.

The rain pounded on the roof, little unseen animals made noises around the windows, and Catty was sure she heard a bear roar. Or maybe it was the lake overflowing its banks and rushing in to drown them all. But those weren't the worst events her imagination came up with. She ground her teeth, wondering what she'd do if he attacked her. Fight back? Run? If so, where to? As usual, she had plunged too impulsively into a good story. She hadn't planned on spending a night alone with him; she'd just got carried away. In the morning, she'd find a way to snoop around. Maybe she could collect enough evidence and make all the suffering worthwhile. The payoff would be a nice, juicy story.

If she didn't get killed first.

When the footsteps did come, Catty was too tired to fight him off—ax or no ax. The fire had died to embers, and she was exhausted from the cold and lack of sleep. She was vaguely conscious of dawn's first light peeping around the edges of the windows as Seth Bernstein's tall, shadowy frame stood over her. She thought she was dreaming when he crouched beside her and put out a hand to brush her hair from her cheek. He said something—just a murmur, really, that didn't scare her, just eased Catty deeper into sleep. Then he gathered her up in his arms, blanket and all. Catty roused herself to mutter a terrible threat meant to scare him off.

She could have sworn he laughed.

His arms felt wonderfully strong and secure, and Catty could hear his breathing as her head rested against his chest. Half asleep, she looped her hands around his neck and let herself be carried. Next thing she knew, she was rolled into the most comfortable bed she'd ever known, and he was tucking her into warm quilts. Then Catty fell deliciously asleep, with the slightest touch of a human hand lingering on her hair. She dreamed. Warm sensations swooped and caressed, her limbs relaxed. The darkness in her mind grew languid and sensual, no longer flashes of frightening past events that had sent a teenage girl fleeing from her home. These images were sweeter, gentler.

She woke to the smell of coffee and a rich, yeasty fragrance wafting in the air, and a vague feeling of disappointment. She was alone, and the sound of rain pattered on the roof over her head.

She didn't feel like getting up too quickly. For a long time, she lay in the quilts and let her thoughts wander—mostly retracing what she could remember about being put to bed and which parts of her dream she could make sense of. She decided Seth must have tucked her in when he went off on his fishing expedition. She sat up and realized she was still wearing her clothes. Obviously, he liked fish more than women.

"I should be grateful I wasn't molested," she muttered. "What time is it?"

She checked her watch and discovered she had slept until noon. That news jolted Catty out of bed like a rocket. Pushing her tangled hair from her face, she padded over to the railing, leaned her elbows there and looked down into the cabin.

Seth was sitting at the table, surrounded by heaps of books and papers, a pair of steel-rimmed glasses on his nose, a pencil tucked behind his ear. But he wasn't studying. He was looking up at her, a cup of coffee suspended halfway to his lips.

"Go ahead," Catty coached. " 'What light from yonder window breaks?' That's your line."

A ghost of a grin crossed his face. He put the cup down. "I was thinking more along some lines I recall about a blind man from Nantucket, but we'll skip over that for now. Sleep well?"

"Once I got up here, yes." Catty descended the steps and ended up sitting on the bottom one. The two dogs dashed up from their snoozing places by the fire and crowded around her, licking Catty's face and shoving at her hands until she petted them. She fondled their ears, but regarded Seth. Even in a frayed sweater and nearly threadbare jeans, he looked noble somehow. Like an exiled prince or something.

She said, "You didn't have to give up your bed for me."

"I didn't do anything as gallant as that. When I got up this morning, you looked pathetic all huddled up on the floor with those dogs. So I took you upstairs." He watched her, his body looking relaxed, but his eyes alert and intense. He said, "I hope you don't mind."

Catty wasn't the type to thank anyone for his kindness, even if he did look like impoverished nobility. So she didn't. Instead, she said, "As long as you behaved yourself, I don't mind a bit."

The grin reappeared—brief, but definitely real. Catty decided that a smile made Seth's face look years younger. He took off his glasses and cast them down across the pages of paper, avoiding her look as if he wanted to keep the unplanned smile to himself.

At that moment, Catty noticed that he'd shaved. His hair was still ragged, but he'd taken the time to scrape the whiskers off his face, and he looked clean-cut. Almost adorable. He had a pronounced dimple along one side of his mouth, she noted. No doubt he'd once been a beautiful baby. Or a ladies' man.

Seth pushed his chair back, then propped both his waffle-soled shoes on the table and clasped his hands loosely behind his head. From that position, he seemed to enjoy the picture she made perched on the step with her hair all over the place and his dogs demanding affection from her. Catty ducked her head and avoided his gaze.

In a moment, he said, "The storm's still in progress, so I didn't go fishing. There's coffee, but that's about it for breakfast until the bread's finished."

"Bread? You're baking bread?"

"Very few supermarkets make deliveries up here. You want to eat, you make it yourself. Can you hold on a little longer?"

Catty's stomach growled at that moment, but she hoped he hadn't heard it. "I'll have an apple. What are you doing?"

He glanced at the paper-strewn table, apparently able to forget instantly that she was a female just fresh from his bed. "Ordering some books, actually. It's the kind of job I save for a rainy day. I figure I have to take you back to civilization as soon as the weather breaks, and I'd like to mail these requests on the same trip. Saves fuel."

"What kind of books are you buying?"

"All kinds. It's going to be a long winter."

Catty got up and shooed the dogs, then went to the table and selected an apple from the bowl. Biting into it, she fingered the book catalogs he'd obviously been thumbing through. Science seemed to be the topic he preferred—biol-

ogy mostly. That and poetry. Looking for further clues, she
tried to be casual.

She became aware of Seth watching her, however. He
didn't move from his relaxed pose, but she knew his attention was riveted upon her. She felt grungy, of course. Her
hair was a tangled mare's nest, she'd washed all her makeup off the night before, and her clothes were not only dirty
from her fall in the woods, they were rumpled now, too. To
top it off, she noticed her fingernail polish had chipped.
And maybe—just maybe—she had started to smell.

Her fragrance must have turned him off suddenly, too, for
abruptly, Seth swung his legs off the table and got up. For
an instant, he towered over her diminutive, sock-footed
frame, and Catty fought to control a hot blush that crept up
her face. *Terrific. I'm alone with Prince Charming and I've
run out of roll-on.* Seth turned and strode into the kitchen.

"I'm going to be busy for a couple of hours," he said
gruffly, pouring himself another cup of coffee from the
plug-in pot on the counter. "There's a lot of paperwork to
get accomplished, and I'd like to get it finished before the
storm quits. I assume you can occupy yourself for a few
hours?"

"Oh, sure." Humiliated, she bit into the apple again.
Around a mouthful, she said, "I've got tons of work to do.
Don't let me get in your way."

He nodded, frowning as he tasted the coffee. "Right."

With her turning pink and looking unforgivably tousled,
Seth felt like a complete ass. She probably thought he was
nuts. He'd come damn close to reaching out and touching
her as she stood beside the table. Had she seen that? The
urge to pull her into his lap and peel off that fuzzy pink
sweater had been overwhelming. *Damn!* Why couldn't he
make himself stop thinking about her that way? In a minute, she was going to notice the change in the shape of his
jeans.

Keep your distance, he commanded himself. So when Catty followed him into the kitchen, he bolted out of her path and made straight for his worktable. He sat down again and realized he was sweating.

How could he let a woman do this to him? He shook his head woefully. One silly female on the premises, and suddenly he was thinking like a sex fiend.

Of course, he couldn't concentrate on his work after that. He tried to focus on the book catalogs, but he kept catching glimpses of Catty out of the corner of his eye. She poured coffee, peeked under the towels at the rising loaves of bread and then proceeded to stroll around the room sipping coffee between bites of apple, unmindful that her presence had sent his senses into a hormonal nosedive.

She took her time studying all the bookshelves, and when she bent over once, Seth realized the seat of her pants was still dusted with dried mud. He nearly groaned. He couldn't tear his gaze away, couldn't even close his eyes and blot out her curving behind.

Trying to intellectualize himself out of that fix, Seth imagined that the mud marks were some kind of Rorschach test, but all he could think about was what lay underneath the fabric. He wondered if he'd forgotten how to get a woman out of her trousers. Had there been any innovations in lingerie since he'd last been in a position to notice?

She turned around and caught him looking again, so Seth manufactured a frown. He *was* feeling angry—with himself, not her, but Catty didn't know that. She spun away hastily. A few minutes later, she escaped out onto the porch.

She stayed outside for nearly a quarter of an hour, and Seth relaxed. *You're an adult,* he lectured himself. *Not a randy teenager.* She'd be gone as soon as the rain stopped. He'd just have to grit his teeth until then.

The lecture didn't help. Catty burst into the cabin from the back door. "Hey!"

Her face shone and her eyes sparkled, and Seth felt his body react as if she'd torn off her clothes and flung herself into his lap. She looked excited and lovely. Her voice vibrated with laughter. "There's a veranda out here!"

He glowered at her. "What?"

She faltered when she saw his expression. "I'm sorry," she said. "I didn't mean to interrupt. I just—I didn't notice this other porch last night. It sticks out over the water. It's really pretty."

"I know," he said. "I live here."

Chagrined only momentarily, Catty snapped, "Well, excuse me for living. I'll shut up now. Go back to work."

He tried. He really did. But most of the afternoon he shuffled papers and rattled the pages of catalogs and couldn't concentrate. First Catty dragged her makeup out of her briefcase and spent fifteen minutes touching up her face in the wicker-framed mirror that hung in the kitchen. Then she spent ten minutes brushing the blond mane of her hair until it gleamed like spun gold. Next she pulled out a bottle of nail polish and curled up on the floor by the fire, painting her nails and blowing on them through puckered-up lips. Seth found that procedure particularly excruciating. He got up from the table and stomped around the kitchen, slamming drawers and dropping utensils and finally jamming two bread pans into the oven to bake. He nearly broke the timer on the stove with the violent wrench he used to set the baking time.

Undoubtedly aware of his pique, Catty quickly located a book on one of the shelves. She curled up on the sofa, opened the novel and settled down with a sigh.

Watching her read would have been easy. Except she pulled off her socks and used her bare feet to massage the dogs, who had begun to act like a pair of lovesick calves over her. As Catty became absorbed in her book, she enslaved the dogs and sent Seth into a frenzy of frustration.

He surged to his feet at last. "I'm going out," he announced, too wrought up to stand another minute alone with her. He strode out the back door, aware of her mystified stare.

He spent an hour storming around in the rain, glaring at the sky and wishing the clouds would dry up and blow away before he did something really stupid. He'd been through some dark times before, but this kind of frustration was different—sharper somehow. More immediate. Why did it have to be *this* woman who had come to his prison? A woman whose *business* was blabbing?

It was ridiculous, really. He'd managed to control himself before—to protect his family, to champion a cause worth any sacrifice. He refused to let himself be undone by an impish little female who just happened to have a luscious mouth and soft skin.

When he returned to the cabin, his disposition unimproved, Seth found Catty still curled up with her book. He saw at once it was a paperback romance novel, probably one his mother had left there years ago. Catty was too caught up in the story to notice his entrance. But when he slammed the door, she started, looking up, and he could see tears glistening in her eyes.

Hastily, she threw the book down and got up, wiping her eyes to obliterate any sign that she'd been weeping over some sappy story.

She stuck her chin out stubbornly and announced, "I'm starving. The timer went off while you were out, so I took the bread out of the oven and now I can't stand it anymore. If you don't want to eat, I'm going ahead without you."

How did she do that? Make him feel like a dope for doing nothing but minding his own business?

"All right," he said. "Let's eat."

He had a jar of peanut butter in a cupboard, which he got out and opened while Catty armed herself with a large knife and began to slice the bread. He slathered first one piece and then another with peanut butter. Catty took hers out onto the rear veranda, and after a moment's hesitation, Seth followed her. The dogs hurried past him and prostrated themselves at Catty's feet.

She sat primly on the steps, watching the rain and eating her food and doing her damnedest to ignore him. Nose upturned, she nibbled the crumbs from her fingers with the daintiness of a kitten. Seth slouched into an Adirondack chair and watched her tongue until he could barely stand it. He could have been eating cardboard for all he knew. He was fascinated.

With her nose tipped still higher in the air, Catty went inside and returned with a second slice of bread for each of them. Seth took her offering without thanking her. Catty turned around and ate her portion while perching on the railing of the veranda, just above the water, her back to him, her bare feet clinging to the bottom rail. Her blond hair stirred in the misty breeze. The rain made a silver curtain before her, Seth thought. Gold on silver, that's what she looked like.

She finished her second piece and licked her fingers all clean. Then, abruptly, she spun around and broke the silence. "Look," she said, "I'm not exactly delighted about being stuck here, you know."

He couldn't answer because of the peanut butter stuck to the roof of his mouth.

"I'd really like to go home," she said, warming up. "I'm not crazy about your life-style, Bernstein. I hate the sleeping arrangements for one thing. The bathroom is unmentionable, too, and your dogs won't leave me alone. The food isn't bad, but the company stinks."

Seth found his voice. "I didn't invite you here."

"No, but you could at least muster some good manners."

"I—"

"I'm not looking for sparkling conversation. I just think you could be a little *nicer*."

"I've been nice. I gave you my bed, didn't I?"

She flushed. Perhaps she remembered more about that episode than she'd let on before. Lucky for him, he'd been able to withstand the urge to crawl into bed with her once he'd rolled her under the covers. She said, "One bed does not a nice person make."

"Oh, for God's sake!"

She said, "You weren't so bad last night. We talked at least! But today—"

"*You* talked last night. I listened."

Her eyes snapped. "Was I boring?"

"Oh, I enjoy hearing about empty-headed celebrities and their ridiculous problems!"

"Don't try to impress me with your intellect, please!" She pointed her finger at him. "I know your type, heartthrob! You're a snob!"

"Where do you get off calling me names? I don't have to be nice to you. It's out of human kindness that I haven't thrown you off this island! You want charming company, go to Hollywood and find a down-and-out actress to kick!"

She stood up, eyes blazing. "I don't have to listen to this! Stay out here and be a grouch! See if I care. I'm going inside to finish my book."

"Take my handkerchief," Seth cracked. "I don't want you sniffling on the pages."

She wheeled on him angrily. "I suppose you never cry over books, do you, Bernstein?"

"You haven't any concept of the things I've cried over."

She braced her hands on her hips. "Try me."

His admission had been reckless. Seth gripped the arms of the chair and vowed he would not be muscled into saying more. Already he felt foolish. Foolish and angry. "Some things are none of your business, Miss Sinclair. I'm not one of your precious celebrities. I'm an ordinary person just like you. I'm not asking about your deprived childhood, am I? I deserve the same courtesy. So lay off!''

She looked angry for a moment, tight-faced and quivering. Suddenly she began to pace. "Okay," she said. "Maybe we've both got a couple of things we'd like to keep to ourselves. Maybe I tend to look at everybody like they're a potential story. But look, I can't stand being ignored!'' Her voice rose and broke. "I'm not a criminal! I'm a person. Don't do this to me, Bernstein.''

Seth felt a pang of guilt. She looked scared and out of place, and he could see that Catty was dying inside. Feeling like a heel, he said, "Don't call me Bernstein.''

"Seth,'' she corrected. Seeing his expression, she begged, "I really can't stand it. I'm a people person. I can't handle you sulking all afternoon. My dad did that all the time and it always ended up with me getting smacked. Give me a break, will you?''

He wanted to know more. The idea of anyone striking Catty appalled him. But it almost explained a few things. Her bluster. The fleeting look of anxiety in her eyes. Her eagerness to be liked.

She tried a smile on him. "Please?''

He let out a sigh. "Okay," he said. "What do you want?''

Her smile trembled at the edges. "Just some attention, that's all. Don't ignore me.'' She climbed up onto the railing again and tried to look happy. She began to chatter in nervous relief. "A bath would be heaven, but that's asking too much. How do you stay clean in this wilderness? When I get back to civilization, I want to soak myself for a week!''

"You want a bath?'' he asked, feeling the wave of recklessness crest and begin to spill inside himself.

"I'd love it.''

Seth looked out at the lake. The rain had stopped. Sometime when he hadn't been paying attention, the downpour had simply ceased. He knew he could get out the boat, pack her into it and take Catty down to Deer Lick before nightfall. But something prevented him—something Seth preferred to ignore for the moment.

Launching himself out of the chair, he grabbed her hand. It was small and warm and felt delightful. He pulled her to her feet. "Let's go."

Three

————

Catty catapulted headlong down the zigzag path beside Seth. She ran, her hand gripped in his, her heart racing. The dogs chased them, barking delightedly. Catty couldn't match Seth's long strides and ended up skidding on the moss, stumbling on the stones. She tugged on his hand, laughing. "Wait, stop!"

"I thought you wanted a bath?"

"I do, but—"

"Come on!"

With a nimbleness surprising in a man so tall, he ducked under the branches of a birch tree and doubled back on the path so that they ended up on a dock that jutted from underneath the cabin's balcony. Catty realized that the rustic cabin had been built on the boulders of a water-filled cave, and the cave served as a boathouse. Breathless, she peered inside and saw the shadow of a fiberglass motorboat bumping gently on its moorings. Stretching from the boathouse onto the lake was a long dock—one in much better repair than the rotting structure Catty had first used to set foot on the island.

Seth released her hand and ducked under the low overhang of the cave. Lightly, he crept along the narrow catwalk until he reached the boat. Catty could hear him rummaging in a footlocker, but she turned away and, still breathing hard, admired the panoramic view.

An eerie mist was rising from the surface of the lake now that the rain had stopped. The still-eddying water looked like molten silver in the dying light of day. Along the shore, the gray silhouettes of tall trees stood like silent phantoms, one after the other growing smaller and smaller until they finally disappeared into the endless horizon of the lake. The storm winds had left quiet waves, which slapped against the rocky shore.

Catty caught her breath and hugged herself, struck by how alone they were on the enormous lake. The air smelled so clear and clean that it made her feel dizzy just to breathe it in. The silence was complete—so unlike the city, that for a moment Catty wondered if she'd somehow landed on another planet. Not even an animal rustled in the trees. Then, far away, a weird cry echoed across the flat lake.

"That's a loon," said Seth, his voice so close in her ear that Catty jumped. "Are you ready?"

She faced him and started to bluster. "What do you have in mind? You don't expect me to go swimming now, do you? In the lake?"

Seth scooped the crook of Catty's arm into his hand and steered her out along the dock. The dogs frisked happily around their legs. "Do you see a hot tub anywhere nearby? Yes, in the lake. You city slickers probably never heard of skinny-dipping, but around here—"

"Skinny-dipping is not a practice totally unknown to me, y'know. I grew up on the ocean."

"Good. Then get out of those clothes and—"

"It's broad daylight!"

"You want to wait until nightfall? When the frogs come out? When the bats start swooping around? When—"

"Okay, okay, you convinced me."

He shoved a dry towel into her hands. The dock bobbed gently underfoot as they paced the length of it, so Seth held onto Catty's arm to keep her steady. When they reached the end of the dock, Catty turned and looked uncertainly up into his face. For a second, she thought about demanding a ride home. Suddenly she wanted to be back in the busy streets, hearing honks and shouts and roaring engines. The last thing she wanted was to strip down with a perfect stranger who might well be a crazed murderer and go for a swim in the huge, eerie lake.

"Listen," she said, fighting off the urge to tell him her worst fears, "this is—I'm not exactly—you see, I—"

He laughed at her. It was such a jolt to see him laugh that Catty found herself staring at him. He had a nice face, a naturally sexy smile. He said, "You're a chicken, is that it?"

"I am not!"

"Then dive in."

"With my clothes on?"

"Your decision," he said, releasing her to haul his ancient sweater over his head. "But judging by your lack of luggage, you're going to be very unhappy if you soak all your clothes for the sake of one unsatisfying bath. You're not as tough as you pretend, are you? Come on. I won't peek, if that's what's got you worried."

"It's not," Catty snapped, stung that he'd seen the truth immediately. But he turned his back to her, and she hastily did the same so that they were facing in opposite directions. As Catty took off her shoes, she heard him drop his sweater on the dock and kick off his shoes. Gripping her towel for dear life, she said tartly, "It's going to be cold, you know. How do you expect to get clean in a cold bath?"

"Quit stalling," he said over his shoulder. "Last one in makes the peanut butter sandwiches."

She heard the jingle of his belt buckle and identified the sound of unzipping jeans. She gulped. "This is very embarrassing, I'll have you know."

"For crying out loud," he said. "We're adults!"

"We're *strangers*."

"Not for long. Come on, Catty. You think I don't know what you've got under that sweater?"

"I *know* you know what I've got, I just don't feel like letting you *see*. I don't go in for this earthy, one-with-nature stuff. I like movies and subways and restaurants and the good, honest smell of a bus driver who smokes cigars! But I—"

"Oh, for heaven's sake," said Seth.

And those were the last words Catty heard before she was picked up by a naked man and thrown into Lake Superior.

She came up sputtering and shouting epithets that would make any Manhattan cabbie blush. The trees rang with the foul names she called him, but by the time she had flung the water from her eyes and opened them, Seth had dived into the water. The dogs joyfully plunged in after him. When he surfaced fifteen yards away, Catty was panting and struggling to stay afloat.

"You're really rotten," she gasped.

"Need help?" he asked sweetly.

"Keep your distance!"

"You're going to have a hard time swimming unless you take off your pants, at least. I could—"

"Stay where you are!" she bellowed. Then she swam clumsily over to the dock and grabbed a handhold. With the sound of Seth's laughter ringing in her ears, she began to rip off her sopping clothes and heave them up onto the dock.

Her sweater landed with a splat, her blouse followed. Catty went on grumbling, but each item of removed clothing was a relief, she had to admit. She was a good swimmer, but her heavy trousers weighed her down significantly. She stripped them off and decided, what the hell, she might as well get rid of her panties and bra, too. At last she was treading water, completely naked and strangely revitalized. Her heart lifted. The lake was warm—warmer than the air, at least, and the fresh, tingling water rushed around her limbs, stealing through her secret places and caressing her skin with sly insistence.

She turned and saw Seth swimming lazily in the deeper water, playing with the retrievers. He swam effortlessly—strong and swift in the water, a friend to the current, smooth as an otter. He flipped onto his back and blew a jet of water into the air, and Catty found herself craning to get a better view, a glimpse of his lean, efficient body.

And suddenly she wanted to be near him. She wanted to see him, and feel the heat his body surely radiated in the water. She wanted to hear Seth laugh again, and she wanted to be near when it happened. She dived underwater to get the weight of her hair streaming out behind her, and then she swam quickly out into the lake. Around him, the dogs splashed merrily.

"Don't drown me," he said when she was close enough to speak to. "You'll never get off this island alive."

"I should duck you." She stopped several feet away to tread water. "That was a mean trick. What am I supposed to wear tonight?"

He grinned, still wrestling with one of the dogs. With his dark hair slicked back, he looked like a pirate. An aristocratic pirate maybe, but still a swashbuckler capable of tossing a willful lady overboard. "We'll find something for you to wear, don't worry. You're not really mad, are you?"

"I should be!"

"You look great," he said, and Catty realized that his black eyes were shining with appreciation as he studied her. She felt sure he couldn't see past the waterline, but he obviously saw something worth admiring. He shoved the dog away and said, "You're beautiful without your makeup."

Ridiculously embarrassed, she summoned a tart voice. "I won't mention your opinion to Marcel next time I go for an appointment."

"Don't," he said softly.

"Don't what?"

"Talk like that."

"I don't know what you mean, so—"

"I like you," he said suddenly. "You're not the cosmopolitan bitch you pretend to be. You're nice. You're—I don't know exactly. Were you really crying over that book this afternoon?"

Catty knew she was blushing and ducked under the water for an instant before answering. She felt strangely giddy, alone with him in the silent water, vulnerable. "I can't help it," she said, avoiding his bemused and curious gaze. "I've got a mushy spot for heroines with sad stories."

"Because you've had one yourself."

"Now, look, Dr. Freud, if you're going to analyze me—"

"I'm sorry," he said. "It's none of my business. But I don't get the chance very often. You're the first woman to turn up here in four years."

"Four years!" Catty splashed water and stared at him, astonished. "You mean you haven't had—I *thought* you were some kind of monk, but I didn't really— Do you mean to tell me you've been celibate for that whole time?"

He laughed. "Painful, but true—unless you count lusting in my heart, which—believe me—doesn't measure up to the real thing. Why do *you* find it so shocking? You don't exactly strike me as the stereotypic single urban female on the prowl for great sex with no commitments.''

''Well, but you're a man. And you're so . . .''

''So what?''

''Sexy,'' Catty said at last, eyeing him warily. ''You know, earthy and natural and—oh, I don't know. I'm sounding stupid, aren't I?''

''I like sex,'' he admitted, casting his head back to look up at the clouded sky. ''At least, I did. I thought I'd forget about it after a while, but it's a human appetite, isn't it? Like food and shelter, it's something people need.''

''Maybe *you* do,'' Catty said, without thinking.

That got his attention. ''You don't like sex?''

''I didn't say that. I just meant—well, it's— What are you smiling about?''

Laughing again, he said, ''I have a feeling about you, Catty Sinclair.''

''What? Wait, I bet I don't want to hear it.''

''Have you ever been in love?''

''No,'' said Catty, like a shot.

''Ever had a lover? Even a short-term one?''

''What are you asking?''

Seth grinned and said, ''How old are you?''

''I'm thirty.''

''I don't believe that.''

''Okay, twenty-nine,'' she said, and when he cocked his eyebrow, she admitted, ''Well, twenty-eight, if you're a stickler for detail.''

''Twenty-eight,'' he said. ''A twenty-eight-year-old virgin.''

''Now just a damned minute! I never said—''

''It's true, isn't it? I knew it.''

His laughter sparked Catty's temper. ''I hate that! Stop it.''

"I'm sorry. I'm laughing at the expression on your face. Why are you so angry? It's not something you're supposed to be ashamed of."

"You *have* been in the wilderness too long," said Catty, mortified that he'd figured out a secret she'd been keeping for an extremely long time. "Look, I'm not terribly proud of it, all right? I mean, a girl can get away with being a rookie for a while, but once you hit twenty-five and haven't done it, people start thinking you're weird. So I just quit mentioning it, you know?"

"And you compensate by acting like the toughest thing in high heels."

"It works," Catty snapped. "Nobody makes fun of me. I really hate being made fun of."

"So I've noticed."

She shot him a quick look to be certain he wasn't laughing at her. "I'm not completely ignorant, of course. I've read the manuals and plenty of sexy novels."

"So you can talk a good game."

"Right. But I'm not—there aren't any guys I feel like doing it with, you know? Sex isn't a big priority with me. Or maybe the right man hasn't shown up yet. I know, that sounds stupid—"

"I think it's charming."

"Charming," Catty repeated, rolling her eyes. "Yeah, right."

"You're special," Seth said.

Catty couldn't look him in the eye. She said, "You're making me blush again."

"I know," he said. "That's charming, too." Then, "I have some soap on the dock. You first?"

She swam slowly away from him. Her head was in a muddle. She felt silly and pleased at the same time. Excited by his compliments, but a little scared, too. Had he seen through her? To the real reason she didn't go looking for sex partners? She couldn't second guess Seth, couldn't imagine what he was really thinking. Maybe he had her completely figured out. That thought worried Catty.

The soap was where he'd promised. Catty dove under the dock and came up on the other side for some privacy. She lathered her body and then her hair, listening to Seth splash as he exercised. The dogs clambered out of the lake and shook themselves off, then flopped down to watch their master swim. In time, Seth returned to the dock, and Catty tossed the soap over to him.

"Still warm enough?" he called to her.

"Yes. I thought the water would be colder."

"It'll cool off quickly now that summer's over," he said, and then proceeded to explain about currents and northwesterly air flows from Canada, warm pockets and the fall equinox. He concluded by saying, "There's a colder current running through this part of the lake right now. Want to feel it?"

Feeling uncharacteristically game, Catty said, "Okay, sure."

"Come on, then." He swam out from the dock and Catty followed. They cruised along at a steady pace, swimming out into the lake away from shore, heads above water to breathe gulps of cold, crisp air. The sky overhead was still gray with clouds, and the light had begun to fade still further. Neither spoke, and as she swam, Catty experienced the strange feeling of entering something—a great abyss, perhaps. The water, the mist and the sky seemed to merge into one silvery-gray element she couldn't put a name to but simply felt. It was liquid, yet airy, warm against her skin but cool on her face and in her lungs. It was a great emptiness.

She could sense the water getting deeper, growing larger around her, and the cool air parted around her face with a soft rushing sound. The quiet grew around them until the only sounds in the world came from their steady strokes.

Catty's heart began to pound. The grayness was complete. The lake became a huge void, and she was but a tiny speck floating in its powerful silence. She stopped swimming and couldn't breathe.

"Seth," she choked, for a moment afraid she was totally alone in the mist.

"I'm here." He checked his speed and turned. In a moment, his head materialized before her. "You okay? A cramp?"

"I'm—I'm scared. It's too deep."

He caught her hand and drew her body toward his. Catty felt his heat, his strength, and seized it, wrapping both arms around his shoulders. She pressed her body to his.

"It's okay," he said, speaking gently to soothe her. He held her snugly against his chest, floating. Her long hair swept around them, streaming out on the water's surface. Their legs tangled for an instant, and Catty struggled to match the rhythm of Seth's easy kick. "You're all right," he said.

"I can't see anything," she said, voice quivering. "Everything's the same color."

"You're all right," he murmured again. "Relax. We're in a current, can you feel it? It's carrying us downstream a little, not dangerous. We'll be in the channel in a minute. It's okay. The dock's just a couple hundred yards that way. Can you hear Sam barking?"

She could, but she clung to Seth, and in the next second she was thankful he was holding her, for the water suddenly changed. The cold enveloped Catty. It seized her body with terrifying completeness. She cried out again. She knew Seth was speaking, trying to calm her, to allay her fear. He talked of weather and water and the cycle of life. In his voice she heard an element of wonder, but she couldn't comprehend his words. She was afraid, disoriented. He kicked gently, propelling them both through the gray emptiness.

"Don't let me go," she begged.

"I won't."

"Hold me. Please, Seth!"

He laughed. "In a minute, I won't be able to let go. Do you realize what you're doing to this poor celibate soul?"

She tried to laugh and hiccuped instead. "I'm scared."

"*I'm* aroused. Who ever decided cold showers were the remedy for desire?"

She couldn't feel a thing. Her body was numb. "I want to go back."

"We're headed that way now." He was telling the truth, for Catty realized they were making steady progress toward the sound of Sam's barking. She could discern the trees through the foggy air, too. But she didn't loosen her embrace. Tensely, she clung to Seth. Even when they passed out of the freezing current and back into the warm part of the lake, Catty didn't relax. She forced herself to breathe again and managed to take in short, painful bursts of air.

"There," he said. "See it?"

The dock loomed, and in another moment, Seth grabbed it. Catty still could not pry her arms from around his neck. She hugged his firm, warm frame, pressing her breasts against his hard chest, her soft belly against his taut one. He felt strange, but secure. He was safety. Her cheek found his, and she clung there, fighting back the urge to cry.

"I'm sorry," he said, one hand slipping up to cup the back of her head through her wet hair. "I shouldn't have taken you out that far."

"I felt so alone!"

"Did you?" Gently, he said, "I don't. When I'm out there, I feel like a part of things—of the whole earth."

"I felt blind!"

He said, "I like not being able to see anything. It makes me look inside myself instead. I'm sorry. I thought you'd feel the same."

She shuddered on a suppressed sob. "I don't like looking inside myself."

He held her a while longer, rocking her gently with the movement of the water. "You're not so bad inside, Catty," he murmured. "Don't be so hard on yourself."

She felt his lips on her temple, then her cheek. His breath warmed her flesh just as his quiet words warmed her mind. At last she allowed him to unwrap her arms from around his neck. "Stay here," he said, fastening her hands to the post of the dock. "I'll get a towel."

He slipped smoothly out of the water and returned ten seconds later to lift Catty from the lake into the cooling air. He wrapped her tightly in a towel, one that smelled slightly of mildew, but it was wonderfully warm and big. He tied a smaller one around his hips and put his arm across Catty's shoulder to lead her up the path to the cabin. The dogs followed, whining anxiously, sensing something wrong. Catty stumbled, hardly able to control her legs.

Indoors, Seth guided Catty to the fireside and eased her down into the nearest chair. She was shivering by then and couldn't stop. He snatched something warm and soft from the couch and wrapped it around her swiftly. He left her for a moment, then returned and pressed a glass into her shaking hands.

"Drink," he said.

Catty's teeth chattered on the edge of the glass. She gulped, expecting wine or some kind of liquor, but it was water. She swallowed convulsively and choked.

She cursed and said, "I ought to rate a real drink, don't you think?"

"This is a real drink."

"I mean booze."

He laughed, sounding relieved to hear her temper rise. "I left my martini shaker at home. No booze for you, young lady. It would send you straight into shock."

"Who says?" she demanded.

"I'm a doctor," he shot back. "I say."

Catty's mind cleared. Maybe it was the sip of water. Maybe it was the truth—words she believed completely for once. She tilted her head and peered up at Seth. He looked momentarily stunned, having admitted something he clearly hadn't intended to let slip. It was obvious that he wished he could snatch back the words. His dark eyes were wide, the rest of his face blank.

"Well, well," Catty said, taking the glass from his hand. "I must be under some new kind of professional medical care. Do many physicians practice in the buff these days?"

The towel was precariously wrapped around his hips, but Seth was still wet and dripped all over the floor. He sent Catty a wry look and straightened, prepared to gloss over his hasty words if she were willing to do the same. He said, "I'll go get some clothes on. You'll be okay?"

She nodded and sipped her water. Seth went up the stairs two at a time and could be heard pulling drawers open and ruffling through clothing. Catty mulled over the information he'd just let slip. In a couple of minutes he came back down dressed in a pair of faded navy drawstring sweatpants, socks and no shirt. He carried a couple of garments over his arms, though, and offered Catty her choice. She pointed, selecting a worn, but comfy-looking rugby shirt. Seth crouched down before her, pulled the blanket from Catty's body and reached, clearly intending to use her towel to rub the rest of the water from her skin before putting the shirt on her.

Catty blocked his hands. "I can dress myself, thanks."

Seth released the towel, but stayed beside her. Gravely, he said, "I'm sorry, you know. About what happened out there. It was my fault, Catty."

She smiled. "No, it wasn't. I'm a grown-up and make my own decisions. I panicked, that's all." She used the end of the towel to rub her hair, but discovered her hands were shaky and stopped. "I nearly drowned you in the process. Sorry about that. I almost deprived the world of a valuable medical man, didn't I?"

He looked pained and took a deep breath. "I shouldn't have said that. I'm not really a physician, but—"

"It's too late to deny it!"

"I'm not denying it," he said doggedly, apparently ready to come clean. "I'm just clarifying. I studied to be a doctor. I finished the schooling, did some research work, but I don't practice."

"Why not?"

"Something," he said, looking her in the eye at last, "came up."

"And?"

"And nothing. I left, that's all. I came here. I don't practice anything anymore."

"Except fishing."

"Except fishing," he agreed.

Catty watched him, seeing how dearly he wanted to end the conversation but believing he also owed her something for causing her to panic in the lake. He was ready to pay for his bad judgment by telling her anything she wanted to know.

And Catty couldn't believe she wasn't asking questions.

But her mind was filled with the many sensations still vivid from the experience in the lake. The hard solidity of Seth's body, his heat, his soothing kindness. She relived the moment when he wrapped the towel around her, inadvertently gathering her body to his own. She remembered details suddenly—the touch of his hand on her skin, the timbre of his voice, the way he matched his steps to hers to guide her safely up the path. Her mouth was dry, her hands still quivered maddeningly in her lap. *What's the problem?*

Whatever she was feeling made it impossible to ask Seth to reveal his secrets.

Seth couldn't believe she wasn't asking, either.

But all she said was, in a somewhat quavery voice, "Would you get my hairbrush, please? It's in my brief-case."

He did as she asked. The brush lay on top of her case, and he carried it to Catty without a word. She took it from his hand and set to work at once, struggling to keep the blanket and wet towel pulled around herself and tug the snarls from her hair at the same time.

Seth stood over her, struck by the picture she made sitting there by the fire, the first woman to enter the cabin in years. Demurely unaware of the effect she made, she attended to her hair. The long, flossy strands hung down her back and had begun to steam gently in the fire's heat. She looked like a fairy-tale princess, a diminutive little figure with a mass of hair, a porcelain face with a sensual mouth. Clasping one tawny lock in her small hand, she ran the glinting bristles of the brush through it time and again. She looked almost angelic sitting there, Seth decided.

But Catty was no angel. The blanket slipped from her shoulders. Seth couldn't forget the way she'd felt against his body—slim and lithe and womanly, her breasts practically branding his chest with their feminine heat. In his mind, he heard the frightened breathlessness in her voice when she'd called for his help and imagined instead how she might cry out in a moment of passion. He had felt the slender strength of her arms as she'd clung to him in the water, but wondered if she'd hold him so tightly in the act of lovemaking.

He reached down and removed the hairbrush from her hand.

Catty spun her head around, her eyes wide, her arms remaining uplifted, as if still holding the brush. Her breasts were motionless, their perfect contour clearly visible through the towel. She kept her knees clamped together—pampered, pretty knees, but as the blanket slipped further, the flesh of her curving thighs shone with the erotic gleam of a harem girl's in the firelight. Seth could see that she was shivering.

He picked up the shirt she'd rejected. "Come on," he said. "You're freezing."

Her eyes looked scared, but she allowed him to slip the shirt over her head. The towel slid to the floor. Seth wanted to see her unclothed again in the golden light, to watch the process of her dressing. But out of conscience, he didn't and cursed himself a moment later for being stupid. He helped her pull her hair out from under the shirt and, with Catty enfolded in the garment, tucked the blanket around her legs, avoiding contact with her skin and longing to caress her.

You should have taken her to Deer Lick as soon as the rain stopped, he lectured himself. Now it was too late. A couple of hours in an open boat, and she'd be one very sick lady. Besides, he wanted to be the one to take care of her.

The hairbrush was still in his hand. Without knowing exactly how, Seth found himself wondering if he dared try untangling her hair. It was clearly her crowning glory, a phrase that seemed a meaningless cliché except where Catty was concerned. Tentatively, he passed the brush down through it. Catty sat quietly. She did not speak as he drew the brush through the strands of her hair a second time. Seth settled into the task then, sometimes tugging, but gradually establishing a rhythm—slow, purposeful. He liked the texture, the way it curled around his fingers. The color glinted in the firelight. It smelled vaguely of the lake, but intoxicatingly of Catty herself.

"You have a gentle touch," she said, tilting her head this way and that as he pulled the brush through.

His mouth felt incredibly dry. He wanted to speak, but couldn't find the words.

She sighed. "It feels wonderful."

He could make her feel wonderful in other ways, too.

Catty made another sound, practically a purr of contentment. Her eyes were half-closed, her mouth curved into a smile that was innocently sensual.

Seth dropped the brush on the chair. He turned Catty by her shoulders and knelt before her, bewitched. Girl and woman. Sure of herself at times, but easily frightened. He touched her face, sliding one finger down the indentation of her cheek, pausing under the rounded point of her chin. The only sound between them was the quiet snap of the fire. Catty opened her eyes, but didn't move. The firelight played over her features.

As if mesmerized, she whispered, "Seth?"

He caressed her throat with his fingertips, brushing her hair out of the way. He could feel her pulse flutter and accelerate. Her breath caught in her throat. Seth couldn't control what happened next. He found himself moving closer, seeking her mouth with his own, pressing deeply into her lips. Catty trembled, but she didn't pull back.

Seth cupped her face, holding her inescapably to his kiss in case she panicked. She tasted sweet, her mouth potent against his. He longed to plunge his tongue inside her, and just barely held that urge in check. Instead, he gyrated her head, finding ways to coax her lips apart. Exquisitely awkward, she finally opened her mouth. Her tongue touched his.

That tiny contact triggered a surge of pleasure. Seth tightened his hold on her. Catty brought up her hand to his chest, her nails skimming his flesh, then weaving into his hair. Seth felt a terrible hunger grow inside himself. He wanted to push the blanket from her knees, spread it on the floor and roll Catty onto it. He wanted to part her legs and kiss her there, too. He wanted to taste her skin, to mouth her breasts, lick the moisture from the downy soft tendril at her temples. He could see himself stroking her thighs, whispering to her, slipping inside and moving swiftly until peace—yes, it was peace, he sought—came to both of them. Kissing her, he saw it all in his mind. He longed to have this woman, to sleep inside her.

But common sense intervened. What was he doing? Seth drew back, his brain finally kicking in. This was the woman who could ruin his life—what little was left of it! Had he gone crazy?

He released her. Catty opened her eyes and blinked.

"I'm sorry," he said. "That was stupid."

Catty cleared her throat, but couldn't manage any words. She looked positively stunned. Or perhaps repulsed.

Seth stood up. He said, "I don't know what got into me."

In a split second, he imagined what could have happened next. He'd have taken her to bed, spent the night making love to her, and the next morning he'd spill every word of the family story. She'd take the next available transportation to New York and alert every branch of the armed forces stationed in the continental United States. And he'd be a dead man in twenty-four hours.

Seth backed up a pace. He drove his fingers through his hair, trying to settle his swirling thoughts. He said, "I'm sorry. That won't happen again."

Catty collected herself, hugging the shirt closer around her body and avoiding his gaze. Her face was flushed—not from arousal, but from embarrassment.

"I'm really sorry. Honestly. It was very rude and—"

She shook her head hastily. "Look, forget it. It was a mistake, okay? I know I'm nothing to get excited about." With a laugh that broke in the middle she said, "Did I mention I was once voted Most Likely to Become a Nun?"

"Catty, I didn't mean—"

"It's okay," she interrupted gruffly. "I'm used to it. No sex is better than sex with me, you know?"

Four

——

Seth swore.

"It's all right," Catty said swiftly. She stood up, shaky but determined not to show any weakness. "You don't have to be kind to me. I've experienced that before, too—a knight in shining armor who thinks I want to become a nymphomaniac. I don't like being a challenge. You don't have to prove how much of a man you are."

"Catty, it's not that I don't find you attractive—"

She laughed coldly and cut him off. "Yeah, I've heard that line before, too. The next word is 'but.' Let's just drop it, okay? I think I want to be alone. Do you mind?" She started past him to terminate the discussion before she broke down and humiliated herself with tears.

"Catty, wait. We've got to talk about this."

She shook off his hand. "No, we don't need to do anything, Dr. Bernstein. No talk, no therapy, no nothing."

"Give me a chance, for God's sake!"

"No, thanks. My sex life is a subject I've gotten very sick of in the past few years, so just—"

He blocked her escape. "Damn it, Catty, I'm talking about my hangups, not yours, all right? Just listen, will you? I won't be manipulated into bed with you just to—"

"Manipulated!" she snapped, incensed.

"Hear me out." Seth's face was set, brows locked dangerously over snapping black eyes. "I feel bad that you've got some kind of complex, but I won't spend the night making love to you to prove you're wrong."

"Don't do me any favors!" She whirled around to shove past him, but Seth grasped her shoulders and stopped her.

"Listen," he commanded, holding her fast. "I'm in trouble, Catty. Surely you've figured that out by now. I wouldn't be spending my life here if I wasn't in some kind of jam, right? Well, the longer you stay here—the closer we get—the worse it could get for you."

"Don't be melodramatic!"

"I have to be," he said. "It's the truth. If I make love to you, Catty, I'm bound to let you inside. Do you understand?"

"N-no."

"I'm sure to let something slip," he said, words spilling faster. "I'll tell you some meaningless bit of information that somebody, somewhere, will want to hear very badly. And that somebody might hurt you to learn what I've told you."

Catty looked up at him, torn between thinking and feeling. She longed to be held in his arms again, to feel his mouth on hers, to breathe with him in heady syncopation once more.

He said, "I can't take you to bed and just—just do it. I can't. It's not a sport for me."

She swallowed. "I'm not asking for anything."

"I know. But I—I'm sorry I kissed you. I'm *not* sorry, but I'm sorry. God, I'm not making sense." He shook his head. "I shouldn't have started anything. It wasn't fair to you."

The pain was clear in his face. Seth was a complex man, a caring one. Catty could see he meant every word.

She took a deep breath for courage. Then, softly, she asked, "Is it bad trouble?"

Seth met her eyes at last. After a moment's hesitation, he nodded. "Yes."

"Someone's looking for you?"

"Yes."

"Did you do something terrible?"

He smiled grimly. "Not to my way of thinking."

"Did you hurt anyone?"

"Hell, no. I want to be sure *nobody* gets hurt. That's my problem. There are people in this world who are in the business of hurting each other."

"Seth, you—you're starting to make *me* feel nervous."

He laughed shortly, ruffling her hair. "That must be an unusual circumstance. I don't think you're nervous very often, Catty."

"Often enough," she said. "But I usually don't admit it."

"I can see that," he said softly. He leaned closer and kissed her on the mouth, their lips brushing once, then parting. It was an instinctive gesture, perhaps he meant it to be a kiss between friends. But his voice grew husky. In a murmur, he said, "I don't want you mixed up in this, Catty. You don't deserve it."

"Maybe I could help."

"You?" He laughed gently. "You're a wildcat in a fight, I'm sure. But this is out of your league."

"How do you know?"

"Don't push it, Catty."

"Pushing is my middle name. I could—"

"The only way you can help me is by doing this." He un-looped her arms that had magically found their way around his neck. "I want to keep my hands off you, Catty. Tomorrow I'll take you to Deer Lick, and you can go back to your life in the city. Continue your search for Rafer Fernando. Forget about me."

"I'm not sure that's possible."

"You're pretty unforgettable yourself," he said, touching her face gently. "You're much more exciting than you realize. I want to hold you, feel you against me. I want to make your body learn a whole repertoire of wonderful sensations. But I can't—not if both of us are going to go on living safe lives. It's a hell of a predicament for a man who's been isolated up here for four years, but it's the way things have to be."

With a last, longing glance down her scantily clad figure, he shook his head and sighed. "A hell of a predicament."

He meant to follow his own rules to the letter, Catty could see. She tried to grin. When she spoke, she was relieved to hear her voice come out sounding almost natural. She said, "I believe you owe me a peanut butter sandwich?"

He smiled again. Resting a hand on her shoulder, he showed every sign of wanting another kiss. But he restrained himself.

"I'll make you something to eat," he said. "But first I'll go get our clothes from the dock. Maybe your things will be dry by morning if I bring them inside."

"Thank you."

When he let himself out of the cabin, Catty leaned against the fireplace and tried to puzzle things out. She felt strange, and for a time she thought the ache was a result of her swim in the lake. But gradually she became aware of the true source of that new sensation—she felt frustrated. Seth had keyed her up somehow, wound her nerves like the spring of a fine watch. And there was no release. And there was more to it than some kind of clumsy sexual longing. Catty wanted to be near him, to hold him and listen to his voice.

"My God," she said aloud. "Am I falling for the guy?"

As if responding to her question, a sudden squawking noise exploded in the cabin. Catty jumped and whirled around, her heart pounding.

"What's that? Seth?"

The squawk sounded again—a grating, metallic noise loud enough to hurt her ears. Catty realized it was coming from the radio on the kitchen counter. Tentatively, she stepped toward the equipment. A red light was flashing above a large switch, so Catty flipped it.

Immediately, a voice filled the cabin. "Bernstein? You there, old buddy? Hey! What's going on over there, big fella? You having any trouble with that visitor of yours? Bernstein? Goddamn, where is that boy? Bernstein? You want me to come pick her up in the morning?"

Frightened by how close the man's voice sounded, Catty cut off the switch, and immediately Kozak's voice was silenced. Then Catty stood there, not breathing, quaking with nervous tension.

Seth was due back in the cabin any second. Without thinking, Catty began to poke and prod all the switches and dials on the radio. Maybe she was going crazy. Or maybe she knew exactly what she was doing. Frantically, she pried the front off the radio and saw a maze of wires and tubes meshed together. Praying she wouldn't be electrocuted, she grabbed one and yanked. It gave way with a satisfying snap. The red light died.

Catty stared at the wire in her hand. "What am I doing? I'm nuts," she muttered to herself, stuffing the wire back into the machine. "I'm really nuts. I could be back in New York making life miserable for an editor!"

But Catty didn't want to go to New York. Not yet. Not until she learned more. About Seth. And about herself. So she sabotaged his radio.

When Seth returned to the cabin, she had the front of the radio back on and was sitting by the fire wondering if she had gone completely crazy.

He fixed her a sandwich and brought her a dish of home-canned peaches, too. Catty took a few bites, then was seized by a fit of hunger and devoured the meal in minutes. Seth appeared to be uninterested in food. He watched her, though, and sipped from a glass of wine. Catty found his gaze flattering. Stimulating, even.

But she was disappointed when he didn't join her on the cushions. He kept his distance. All evening, he watched and listened to her chatter, but he didn't come any closer.

At last, Catty grew sleepy. Her eyelids felt heavy, and she even lost interest in telling Seth about her misadventures with a Los Angeles press agent.

He took her dishes away and washed them in the kitchen. When he returned, Catty was almost dozing by the fire. Seth gathered her up in his arms.

"Wait," Catty grumbled. "I can walk."

"You can barely keep your eyes open. I'm taking you to bed."

As he began to mount the steps, Catty protested drowsily. "You're not planning to give up your bed tonight, are you? Honestly, I feel terrible about putting you out—"

"Shut up," he said, but his voice was gentle.

Catty subsided in his arms, reveling in the contented feeling elicited just by the sound of his heartbeat against her ear. She'd never felt so at home with a man—so relaxed. When he placed her into the tumble of quilts, she was nearly asleep. But she reached out and stopped him when he started to draw back.

"Wait, Seth."

He hesitated, clearly torn between the urge to climb into the bed with Catty and running down the stairs to escape her.

Catty smiled. "Please don't make me feel like a jerk. Stay. Sleep here tonight. I'll keep my hands off you, I promise."

He laughed, his gaze warm upon her. "That's hardly the problem."

"How about if I vow to fight like hell if you put one finger on me?"

He sighed. "Catty—"

"I mean it," she coaxed. "If there's one bed, we've got to share it. Otherwise, I'm taking the floor again."

"Don't be foolish. I'm perfectly happy to sleep downstairs."

She struggled to sit up. "Then I'm going with you."

"Lie down!" He braced his hands on her arms, then let go as if she'd burned him. He said, "You need a good night's rest. You've had a bad experience."

"Then don't give me another one. Stay."

He bundled her into the bedclothes. "Stubborn witch," he said severely, then took another look at her face and melted. "I've got things to do before I hit the sack. Go to sleep."

"You'll come back?"

"Don't you ever give up, woman?"

"Never. Promise you won't sleep on the floor."

He shook his head, bemused by her insistence. "I won't promise anything. Say good night, Gracie."

Catty yawned. Then, obediently, she murmured, "Good night, Gracie."

Sleep overwhelmed her as she listened to the quiet noises he made, moving around the cabin, taking care of the dogs, adding wood to the fire. She liked the feeling, though, that he was near.

Catty didn't remember the moment she realized he was back, but sometime in the night, Seth did join her. He rolled stealthily in beside her and relaxed on the farthest edge of the bed, trying not to disturb her. Catty didn't wake—not exactly. She was only aware that at last she wasn't alone. Slipping closer to his warmth, she snuggled until her head was tucked under his chin, and she could hear the steady thump of his heart. She heard him groan, too, but that didn't matter. She breathed a contented sigh across his bare chest and fell back to sleep, thoughts scattering like stardust.

In the morning, she woke to a soft caress. Like a warm breeze, Seth moved his hand on her skin, along the curve of her thigh from hip to knee. Perhaps he was still asleep, unaware of what he'd done, because his breathing didn't change. But Catty woke. She didn't dare open her eyes and turn her head for fear the dreamy quality of the early morning might be broken. She lay very still and wondered if he'd do it again. Her own breathing quickened. A fine perspiration sprang out on her skin. The bed felt so warm that suddenly she wondered if she weren't feverish.

To cool off, she moved her foot to push the quilt off her legs. Seth stirred and shifted, startling Catty into freezing. But he simply turned onto his back with a long breath that signified how soundly he still slept. Catty rolled onto her stomach and propped her chin in her cupped hand to look at Seth in the half light of early dawn.

His face wasn't quite so solemn in response as it was when he was awake, she decided. Whatever trouble he was in clearly weighed heavily upon him. But asleep, he looked different—less tense, of course, but younger, too. Sexier, yes, but that word didn't quite suffice either.

He was a sensual man, she decided. He used all his senses to partake of the world around him. Catty remembered how easily he'd enjoyed the lake, for instance. He'd floated in the water with his eyes closed, not fearing, but experiencing the elements around him. When he'd drunk his wine, he'd tasted every subtlety of each mouthful. When he'd kissed Catty, she'd felt him drink in everything about her.

She touched his chest lightly, tracing the shape of his bones and muscles with the tips of her fingers. He was at once strong and vulnerable, a man with a disquieting inner power, but weaknesses, too. And he had been so wonderfully tender with her.

Gently, she pushed the quilt aside so she could admire his body—the shape of his belly, the way the crisp hair on his chest spiraled downwards. With the most wisping of tentative caresses, she passed her fingers down his stomach and under the warm cover of the quilt. Smiling, she discovered he was wearing a pair of very soft flannel pajama bottoms. Through the thin fabric, she found the shape of his hip, the hard strength of his thigh. Growing bolder, she slid inside the drawstring waistband. She ventured slowly downward. At last she encountered the heat of him and felt his pulse beating in her hand. The pulse grew stronger, and Catty wondered at the instinctive nature of man, how easily the mind could be betrayed by flesh.

Her own body reacted, too, filling with sensations Catty didn't completely recognize. She felt affection for him. Respect, too. But something stronger also quivered along her nerve endings. She tingled with excitement but felt a wonderful laziness at the same time. Catty's legs felt heavy, but acutely alive. Deep inside, she experienced a coiling kind of pleasure so strong she found she could only take in shallow breaths of air. Against the palm of her hand, Seth grew taut.

Braver still, she began to caress him.

She cried out when Seth seized her wrist.

Awake, he moved quick as a cat, pinning Catty flat on her back, arms caught over her head on the pillow. She laughed, but he was growling.

"What the hell are you doing?"

"I'm sorry!" She smiled up into his forbidding face. "I was curious—just exploring a little."

"Amateur exploring can get you into trouble." His voice sounded threatening, but Catty could see the threat was empty. Different emotions played across Seth's features. His eyes burned with an erotic fire.

Deftly, he trapped her right knee and settled provocatively between her thighs. Catty could feel the rigid power of his legs, the easy strength in his hips as he rode against her. But most of all, she felt the unmistakable thrust of his arousal against her own most vulnerable place.

"Quit smiling," Seth ordered.

"Why?"

"Because you're too damn beautiful and I— Oh, for God's sake!"

Full of second thoughts he started to roll away from her, but Catty caught him in her arms and held on. "Wait," she said, laughing again. "I like it."

"I can see you like it," he snapped. "I like it, too. Too much! How often do you suppose I wake up like that? Catty, maybe you don't understand some important facts about the male of the species. In another minute—"

"Let's not wait another minute."

He stared at her, his grip slackened. Catty slid her wrists free and wound her arms around his neck.

"Listen," she said, tugging playfully at his ear. "I heard every word you said last night. Really, I did. You're worried about things I don't understand, and I'm willing to accept that. But we could still—I mean, why not? I like you. It might be fun, and—"

"It would be more than fun," Seth said darkly.

"Then let's," she whispered, managing a smile.

A shade of a smile began to tease the corners of his mouth, too. "What's gotten into you this morning?"

"I don't know," she admitted, voice trembling a little. "I feel almost like this is a dream—something that's not quite real. Inside there's—I feel different. Relaxed, I guess. Happy. You're a good man, Seth Bernstein. I wish you'd be the first for me."

"Catty—"

"I know, sex isn't a sport for you. I don't want gymnastics. But I've got something to share, something to give. And I think you'd know what to do with it."

Seth moved against her, a deliberate thrust that hinted at how much energy boiled inside of him. Catty gasped.

"How much do you want to give?"

"I don't know. I—"

"I want everything, Catty. Not just your body. Everything."

"Then take it," she whispered. "I want somebody to know me—everything about me. Not just the face I put on."

He touched her face, forcing Catty to open her eyes and look at him. Seriously, he said, "I thought you didn't like looking inside yourself."

"I don't. At least, I haven't in the past." She chewed her lip for a moment, then came clean. "I haven't led the best life, Seth, I know. I've done things I should be ashamed of."

He stroked her through the shirt, tantalizing her with a touch that promised more. "Like what?"

She swallowed. She knew he was extracting a price. Before he could make love, he needed to understand her. Before there was physical closeness, there had to be emotional closeness, and Catty knew she would have to open up. "Like writing stories when I haven't double-checked my facts," she said. "Like stretching the truth to make it sound better."

Softly, his mouth skimming the fabric of the shirt she wore, just above the curve of her breast, he asked, "Why?"

"To make my stories better. To make more money. To have some prestige. I need those things, Seth."

"Do you?"

She was trembling, but the words spilled out anyway. "I came from a terrible place, Seth."

He lifted his head and looked her in the eye. "Was it the place that was so bad?"

"What do you mean?"

"Usually it's the people that make the difference."

"Oh. You mean—you're asking about my father."

"You want to tell me about him?"

She shook her head convulsively. "No, I— Things are pretty messed up where he's concerned."

Seth rolled up onto his elbow. Slowly, he caressed Catty. "Talk to me."

"You wouldn't understand. You're very different from my father."

"How?"

"Oh, a hundred ways."

"You said before that he used to hit you."

So this was what Seth meant by giving. Catty felt uneasy, but for once she thought she might be able to verbalize what had happened long ago. "Well, he—yeah. He did hit me. It started when I was twelve, when my sister left home."

"You have a sister? What's her name?"

"Nina. She was my father's pet, the pretty one, the smart one." Catty smiled nervously, but couldn't maintain it. "My father adored her. But she—she went into the kind of life most of the girls in our neighborhood went into. You probably don't have any idea—"

"I can guess," he said, settling beside her, abandoning seduction to hold her and listen.

Catty rested her head against his shoulder. The story of her youth was something she'd never shared with anyone. In fact, she'd spent a great many hours of her adult life trying to eradicate every memory of her early years. But suddenly the images were alive in her mind. She could remember the scenes as clearly as if they'd just occurred.

She continued slowly, "Nina started sneaking out at night when she was fifteen. We shared a bedroom, and she'd go out the window. I never said a word, not even when my mother found out. We all kept quiet for fear of what he'd do. But he figured it out for himself, even though he was drunk most of the time. Nina had money all of a sudden, nice clothes and—"

She stumbled on the next words. Seth kissed her face, and Catty realized he was kissing tears. He did not try to stop the flow, but rather to ease them from her. She held Seth tightly against her body, arms hugging his shoulders. "My father found fifty dollars in Nina's purse. That was a fortune for us! It happened a few days after Christmas, I remember. He beat Nina, broke her nose and threw her out of the apartment. He never hit her before."

She took a deep breath. "Nina never came back."

"Catty, love." Seth murmured, wrapping her arms around her shaking body.

"I love my sister," she burst out. "I really do. She was sweet to me. I didn't care what she'd become, but my dad, he was off the deep end about it."

"He didn't want the same thing to happen to you."

"Right. He kept track of my comings and goings like I was some kind of prisoner."

"That must have been tough for you. You like your independence."

"Yes, I always have. Naturally, I broke out of jail once in a while. I made friends with one of Nina's old boyfriends."

"Did your father know?"

"Hell, no." Catty laughed unsteadily. "But there was one night . . ."

"What happened?"

"No," Catty said quickly, edging away from him. "Listen, this can't possibly be interesting."

"Tell me," Seth murmured, catching her gently. "I want to know, Catty. What happened?"

Catty found she was shivering. Her memory was vivid. She could almost hear the sounds—the rain slapping the sidewalks, the raspy grunts of the boy who tried to force her, her own terrified breathing and the frightened sound of choked-back screams. She hid her face in her hands.

Seth's touch turned firm and comforting. His voice was like a caress. "Tell me."

"It—this isn't easy."

"Did someone hurt you?"

Catty nodded. "I made a date with Nina's friend. We—I had to sneak out of the house. He brought some beer and thought I was—well, he thought we should take off our clothes and—and—"

"It's okay," Seth murmured. "It's over now."

"I fought him," Catty said. "I really did. He scared the daylights out of me, but I—I got away. I ran home in the rain, my sweater torn, mud on my face. I was scared to death—that was my introduction to sex! I must have looked—well, my dad took one look and hit the roof."

"But it wasn't your fault."

"That's not the way he figured it. He beat me up. I don't know which was worse—my father hitting me and yelling at me or that boy trying to—to—"

"Rape you."

Even the word sounded terrible. Catty looked away. "I couldn't—I didn't want to go to school because of the bruises. From the way I looked, I knew all my friends would figure out what had happened. But he made me go. He took me himself so he could be sure I walked in the front door every day until my face healed."

Seth uttered a soft curse. "Hitting you wasn't enough? He had to humiliate you, too."

Catty nodded and tried to control her voice. "My father said he'd kill me before I started to earn my living on my back."

"You must have been desperate to get away from him."

She took a deep breath and tried to calm down. "Oh, I was. But we were so poor. I started to deliver newspapers. After a while, the paper hired me to run errands, so I took the job. I lied about my age, and pretty soon I was writing obits. I moved out of the house, but I sent money to him for years after that, even after my mother died. I don't know why."

"You wanted to make him proud of you. To prove yourself."

"No," said Catty. She dashed the tears from her face.

"Then why?"

"I don't know. I just—I wanted to get away from him, that's all. I wanted to make something of myself and never go back."

"You haven't gone back?"

"He's dead," she said firmly. "I heard about it from a neighbor I met by chance in Grand Central. He'd been dead for two years and I never knew it."

"What about your sister?"

Catty put her face against his shoulder, determined not to lose her self-control all over again. "She's okay. In and out of clinics, but she's—she's going to make it. She changed her life. She makes me ashamed sometimes."

"For heaven's sake, why?"

"She's been through so much, and she's still so strong. And I—well, I've taken the cheap route, haven't I? Every now and then I try to write about Nina. I think her story would help some people. But I can't do it. I haven't got the talent."

"What do you mean? You make a good living at writing."

"But not—Nina's story is different. I haven't got what it takes to write good stuff like that. My dad used to say that Nina was the star. I figured I'd never amount to anything. I guess I still think that way."

Seth held her. For a long while he said nothing, just rocked Catty gently in the bedclothes while she choked back more tears. "Go ahead and cry," he said. "Let it go, Catty." When she allowed herself to weep and the storm had passed, he said at last, "I wish I could change things."

"I don't," Catty retorted, mustering some of her usual bluster. "If things had been different, I wouldn't be so tough. I like myself."

"Do you?"

"Most of the time," she amended. "I admit I've got a few problems."

He used a forefinger to wipe the last tears from her cheek. "Such as?"

She tried to smile. "Well, we both know I'm probably going to turn out to be one of the most repressed spinsters in history, so—"

"No," he said. "You're not completely repressed. You were nearly raped. And if that wasn't bad enough, you were punished for something you didn't do. It wasn't fair. No wonder you're still steering clear of sex."

She laughed nervously. "Is that your professional opinion, Dr. Bernstein?"

He took a deep breath and looked into her eyes. "My name," he said, "isn't Bernstein."

Catty stared up at him, unable to respond. How had this happened? She told him her biggest secrets and suddenly he wanted to reciprocate.

Seth bulldozed ahead, saying, "I'm Seth Barnhurst and I'm a research biochemist. I don't think you're repressed,

Catty, I think you're frightened. Of yourself mostly, but of the past, too. The past we can't change, but the rest—look, you're a beautiful woman."

"Oh, don't—"

"It's true. Don't belittle yourself. You've got wit and charm, not to mention the most tempting body I've seen in years—"

Shaken, Catty tried to be funny. "What kind of a compliment is that? You haven't laid eyes on anything but fish and your friend Kozak for years, have you?"

He grinned and looked wonderfully handsome in that soft light. And Catty felt her heart expand within her chest. How had this happened, she wondered? How had she found a man so sweet and gentle, who understood so easily?

Seth said, "I don't think I can keep my hands off you."

"Why try?" she asked softly, her pulse tearing out of control. "What's stopping you, Dr. Barnhurst?"

He looked at her steadily. "Are you sure?"

"I've had a few bad experiences." With difficulty, Catty said, "I've been afraid to try again. I haven't been able to—to—"

"To trust anyone?"

Shyly, she nodded. "I guess that's it."

Solemn, Seth said, "I won't hurt you, Catty."

"I know that. You're sweet. You're—I don't know, exactly. I'm amazed that I feel so comfortable with you. I've known you for such a short time, but I—I keep thinking about us like this."

"Like this?"

"In bed together. Do you want to undress me?"

Seth smiled and caught the hem of the rugby shirt that had become hopelessly twisted around Catty's torso. "Very much. But my conscience is trying to stop me. I want to make this special for you, Catty."

"It is special. You make me feel—I'm not sure. Excited and scared, but—but like you think I'm all right."

"You're more than all right. You're beautiful. And sexier than you know." He knotted his fists in the shirt. "Catty, I want you, too. But it's obvious that my life is a mess. I can't declare my love and carry you off to live in a condo on the Upper East Side. I—"

"I'm not asking for promises." She wound her arms around his neck and tipped her mouth up to his. "I think it could be right, that's all." She kissed him, then looked up into his eyes. "Shall we?"

He groaned and surrendered. In an instant the shirt was up over Catty's head and there was fire in Seth's eyes again when he gazed at her body. Catty blushed and caught her hair in her hands in an effort to shield herself from his hungry stare.

Gently, he pulled her hands back. "Don't," he said. "Let me see you."

"I'm nervous again."

"It's not nerves, love. It's desire you're feeling. See?" He touched her breast, rolling the nipple with exquisite gentleness between his fingers. Catty gasped, and the throaty sound that escaped her lips made Seth smile.

He nibbled her earlobes, then whispered exactly what he wanted to do with her. Hearing him say it made Catty blush all over again, though they were certainly words she'd heard before in a different context. He curled one arm under the nape of her neck, and his other hand skated down her body, cupping her breast, fanning across her belly. And finally delving between her thighs. He avoided her sensitive flesh, just drew small, tantalizing circles on the soft skin of her legs.

In time, growing dizzy, Catty reached to touch him, but Seth caught her hand and brought it to his lips. Unhurried, he kissed her palm, then transferred his mouth to hers. Catty wound her arms around his neck, pulling him deeply into the kiss. Her head swam. She felt her heart pounding.

She tried to listen when he spoke, but Seth had to repeat himself. "You're not on the pill, are you?"

"No, of course not."

"Then you know," he said, "that you could get pregnant."

Catty gulped, for the thought hadn't exactly been at the forefront of her mind. "Well, I— Oh, dear, what now? I've gone and spoiled things—"

Seth grinned. "You haven't done a thing. It's the way the world works, love. I'm afraid contraceptives aren't exactly on my list of regular supplies, so—now, don't look so desperate. There are plenty of things we can do, you know."

"Show me," Catty said, reaching hesitantly for the drawstring on his pajamas. She tried to smile. "Tell me what to do."

"Do what you like," he told her.

She did. Tentatively at first. But gradually with pleasure. She loved looking at his body, and touched and caressed and laughed when she triggered a response. Seth took over soon, though. If perhaps he grew exasperated with her inexperience, he didn't let it show. He tumbled her onto her belly and teased Catty's neck with kisses. He massaged the slender muscles of her back and tantalized the round curves of her backside. He smoothed his hands up and down her slim legs, learning their contour, searching out the sensitive spots behind her knees. They wrestled, caressed. They were tender, then rough. Their laughter soon turned to hoarser sounds, their actions became swifter. And at last Catty found herself crying out as sensations blossomed inside her, nurtured by his hands, his mouth, growing more unbearably wonderful by the moment.

"Let go," he murmured, adding softer words lost amid the swell of rushing blood in Catty's ears.

She clutched at him, seized the bedclothes in her fists, fought the inexorable pleasure until at last she felt as though she had been thrust atop a dizzying peak. She lingered there, on the edge, struggling against herself, against the strumming of her body. Then the mountaintop exploded and Catty felt herself launched into space. Undammed, her passions cascaded in a storm.

Seth swiftly slid up her body and smothered her cries with his own mouth. When Catty opened her eyes, she found his gaze upon her—very intense, pupils dilated. She flung her arms around him, laughing and weeping at the same time. Pressing her warm body against his, she said his name over and over, as if committing the sound of it to the act she had just experienced. She luxuriated in the lithe power of his body, the thrust of his still-aroused condition hot between them. Instinctively, she moved her hips to ride against him. Seth's breath rasped in his throat. He gripped handfuls of her hair. Catty dug her fingers into the smooth muscle of his back and undulated beneath him, longing to reach his soul, to make him tremble as she had.

"Stop," he begged at last. "Have mercy, will you?" He tried to disengage himself from her arms. "There are limits to my powers of restraint. Another minute and I won't be able to control myself. My God, you're a responsive wench!"

"Then don't try to control yourself. I want to give you pleasure, Seth. I don't care about the consequences."

He twisted sharply to avoid her touch. "Then it's lucky one of us has a clear head. You'd regret it plenty if—for pity's sake, Catty! Stop that!"

She obeyed, but not because of his command. Suddenly the cabin was filled with the noise of barking. Downstairs, the dogs were leaping at the back door, raising a ruckus.

Seth sat up on one elbow. "What the hell?"

"What's the matter?"

"Oh, no," he said, galvanized off the bed. "There's only one man alive who's got such a miserable sense of timing."

"What are you talking about?" Catty stared as her lover leaped up and snatched his jeans from the bedpost. "What's happening?"

"It's Kozak," Seth said, hauling on his pants. "Darling, it's unforgivable, I know, but—"

"You mean he's here? *Now?*"

"Yes. And unless you don't care if he finds you looking naked and satisfied, you'd better get up." Seth grinned and bent over her, bracing his hands on either side of Catty's still-reclining body. He kissed her hard on the mouth, swiping his tongue ardently across hers. Then he looked deeply into her eyes. "I don't know whether I should thank him for coming at this fateful moment or send him packing."

"Do I get a vote?" Catty asked, smiling shakily.

"No." Seth kissed her again. "Now get dressed while I stall him outside."

Catty sat up and seized Seth's hand, preventing him from leaving the loft. "Wait," she said. "What will it take to make him go away?"

Seth laughed. "Are you kidding?"

"If you think I'll be content to pack my briefcase and go quietly, you don't know me very well. Please, Seth. Bribe him or something. I—I can't leave like this." She clambered to her knees, her hair skimming her shoulders, teasing her skin. She placed his hand under her breast to feel its weight fully in his palm. "Don't send me away."

He stared hungrily at her body and impulsively ran his thumb over her already erect nipple. Desire was clearly carved in his face, and for an instant Catty thought he might bend closer and press his mouth against her breast. But he checked that urge. "Don't worry," he said in a growl. "I have no intention of letting you go. Not yet."

Five

Seth slid into his shoes and hustled a shirt over his head as he burst out the door and onto the porch. Sam and Betsy surged past him, joyously barking their heads off. They loved Mike Kozak. With their sensitive ears, they could hear the resonant roar of his boat's diesel engines for miles before he actually arrived. Fortunately, they had detected the sound early this morning, too, so Seth reached the dock before Kozak rounded the point of the island in a dazzle of sunlight on the water. Feeling relatively composed, Seth lifted his hand to wave.

"Damn it," Kozak cheerfully shouted when the boat drew within hailing distance. "Haven't you got any bumpers on that dock yet? You'll ruin my baby!"

Seth laughed. Kozak's boat was a beautifully sleek wooden craft once used to ferry passengers around the locks at Sault Ste. Marie. Kozak had found the boat in a deserted yard many years ago, and he'd spent months lovingly restoring the fine teak hull. The struggle to overhaul and maintain her temperamental engines was an ongoing job of which Kozak never seemed to tire. As a result, his boat was a handsome, majestic craft that grandly toured the islands of the lake in fair weather and foul so that Kozak could supply food and equipment to the far-flung residents in the loosely knit community. So regal did the boat look that Kozak referred to her as Queen Victoria. Seth suspected the name also reflected Kozak's private belief that his boat had a personality—and so omnipotent that only the name of an equally powerful but temperamental queen could suffice.

Kozak cut the engines and allowed his queen to coast into the dock.

Seth liked Mike Kozak and was usually delighted to see him. He plastered a fairly good imitation of a welcome smile and with practiced expertise, caught the bow of the Queen Victoria as she sailed by. He threw his weight into deflecting her from the dock, and the boat turned smoothly, then touched the dock with her gunwales as gently as a kiss.

Kozak leaped out, line in hand, which he slipped through a mooring ring on the dock. With a sharp yank, he secured the boat. The dogs jumped up on him, tails wagging frantically.

"You won't believe it," Kozak said to Seth. "I just saw a bear swimming in the lake. It was like some kind of Shakespearean sign."

Seth laughed. "You trying to scare me off this island?"

"I could do better than a bear story if I put my mind to it. I'm relieved to see you're alive." With a grin, Kozak shoved the dogs away, then pulled off one of his oil-stained gloves.

Seth tied the bowline and put out his hand to shake Kozak's. "Afraid the fish finally got me?"

"No, I thought you'd be dead of exhaustion—from entertaining your female guest, of course. You do look pretty terrible. She still here? Did I come at a bad time?'' He waggled his eyebrow salaciously.

"What makes you think she's the least bit desirable?'' Seth demanded. "Maybe she's seventy years old and—''

Kozak laughed. "Don't give me that! I can see by your face she's not. That, and your shirt's inside out.''

Seth started to flush. Kozak saw his expression and howled. Which made Seth even angrier with himself. "Now just a minute—''

"Don't try to hide anything from me. I can guess what you were doing—or attempting to do. You forget how, old buddy? Or maybe she's tired of you already?'' Turning hopefully toward the cabin, Kozak said, "I'm a nice guy, maybe I'll offer to take her back to my place before I return her to civilization for you. She might like to see my etchings.''

Seth caught his arm. "You haven't got any etchings. Just put your dirty mind on hold, will you?''

Seth had known Kozak since the first month Seth arrived on the lake to stay, on a November night when the Queen Victoria was at her most ornery. Her engines quit while she was still miles out on the lake. Seth had seen Kozak's distress light and gone to investigate. That blustery night was the beginning of a beautiful friendship, the closest friendship Seth had ever experienced.

"Dirty mind?'' Kozak complained, affronted. "Have you ever known anybody with a cleaner one than me? Why, I'm more pure than *you* are! At least I get to exercise my fantasies once in a while to cleanse my soul, but you haven't seen a woman in—''

"Cleansing your soul?'' Seth laughed. "Is that what Margaret calls it?''

"She left,'' Kozak said, pulling off his other glove. He avoided Seth's look of inquiry by squinting up at the cabin in the blaze of early sunlight. "And no, that wasn't what she called it."

"She left?" Seth repeated.

"Yeah, went back to Seattle."

"I'm sorry, Mike."

Kozak grinned. "It was fun while it lasted. I liked her, but—" He lifted his shoulders in a life-goes-on shrug.

Mike Kozak was probably not the kind of man Seth would have befriended if he'd still been living in the real world. Kozak was a Vietnam vet who had quit college in his freshman year to fly missions in a war every other member of his family vehemently protested. Like many vets returning from the most horrific experience of their lives, Kozak hadn't gotten his life in order very quickly. He'd hit the bottle, and his battle with booze took him further down in the world than most people ever imagined. Finally landing on a campsite on Lake Superior, though, Mike bottomed out and began the long, slow process of pulling himself together. He quit alcohol and started to carve a place in a community that was unconventional perhaps, but comfortable for a man like him. He used his boat and his pontoon plane to carry goods to other island-dwellers within a fifty-mile radius.

Like Seth, Mike Kozak had something to fear from civilization. But Mike's worst nightmare started with a bottle. He'd stayed sober, but Seth knew he constantly worried about going back to drinking. One night in March he'd come across the lake—ostensibly to give Seth some flour and fresh milk, but he'd quickly agreed to stay the night when Seth offered. Clearly, he needed some companionship to help him through an especially tough period. Over coffee at the fireside, he finally told Seth about his past, about his trouble with drinking. Perhaps it was foolish, but Seth responded in kind. He'd told Kozak about the mess he'd made of his own life—not all the details, perhaps, but enough so Kozak understood he was trusted.

Seth's confession had had an effect on Kozak. It had scared the hell out of him.

He'd said, "What if I get loaded and tell somebody what you've just told me?"

"You won't," said Seth.

Kozak looked frightened in the firelight—a big man gone pale and trembling. "I might."

"No," Seth told him. "I trust you."

Kozak turned away, and a moment later put his face into his hands. He wept. In time, he pulled himself together. "Nobody's said that to me in a long time. I won't betray you. I promise."

It had been a promise he'd kept. Kozak stayed away from liquor. He admitted that a day didn't pass when he wondered if he'd make it without a drink, but so far he'd managed. His life took a swing upward.

He began to have relationships with other people besides Seth. Even women. His affairs were few and far between simply because of his isolated location, but once in a while he found someone to share his bed in the house he started to build across the channel. Margaret Strum had been his latest girlfriend, a college professor on sabbatical to study the Indians who had once populated Lake Superior. With his intimate knowledge of the lake and islands, Mike had helped her locate some artifacts, and they'd spent the winter cataloging their finds. Now, it seemed, Margaret had gone back to her school.

"Is she going to write to you?" Seth asked.

"Sure. We agreed to be friends. You know how it goes. She's got a live-in at the college, a guy she thinks she wants to marry. I knew about him before we got started."

Seth touched his shoulder. "You okay?"

Kozak looked him in the eye and guessed what Seth was asking. "Yeah," he said. "I'm all right."

"I didn't mean if you were drinking. I only—"

"I know. Listen, it's no big deal. I'm a free man again, that's all. Which means, my friend, that I'll be happy to take the little lady off your hands now. She's obviously too much for you to handle."

"Stuff it," Seth said, and Kozak laughed.

He choked on his laughter the next minute, however, when he tilted his head back and saw Catty on the balcony above them. She was leaning on her elbows, her small, mischievous face surrounded by the blond mop of her hair, which caught the morning rays and glinted with pinpoints of sunlight. She had put on Seth's rugby shirt again, but her legs were bare from the knees down, and the view from the dock below was enough to render Seth suddenly very weak in his own knees.

She smiled at the two dumbstruck men. "Hi, there," she called down to them. "You must be Kozak."

Kozak whimpered a comic prayer and shot Seth a look of complete disbelief. Then he lifted his face and called, "Yes, ma'am. And whom do I have the distinct pleasure of addressing this fine morning?"

Seth groaned. "Mike, this is Catty. Catty Sinclair is her name. Catty, this is my—my what? I hesitate to call him my friend at the moment while he's drooling on my shoes, but he's Mike Kozak."

Catty smiled some more. "Hi," she said again, and the soft vibration of laughter in her voice sent a shiver of pleasure up Seth's spine.

"Wait right there," Kozak said, obviously reacting to her voice the same way Seth had. He started purposefully for the zigzag path. "I'm coming up to make sure you're for real."

Seth grabbed his elbow. "She's for real, all right. You don't need to verify it."

"Oho," said Kozak, dropping his voice so his next words were only between the two of them. "Then there *is* something going on here? What have I interrupted, Seth? You two playing mommy bear and daddy bear? She looks delicious. Just let me lick her neck, will you? Then I promise I'll—"

"Catty," Seth called to her. "Why don't you run along for a while? I'm going to throw this man in the lake to cool him off, and I don't want you to hear the language he'll undoubtably use."

Laughing, Catty departed as she was told, heading for the bathhouse. She had a towel and her briefcase, so Seth assumed she was heading to wash up.

"You're a spoilsport," Kozak complained. "At least give me a cup of coffee, will you? So I can get a closer look at her? My God, she's gorgeous! I might as well take a look at your radio, too while I'm here. Why don't we—"

"Checking my radio is the flimsiest excuse I ever heard of!"

"I'm not checking it, I'm fixing it. Didn't you know it was broken?"

"What are you talking about?"

"I've been trying to raise you since yesterday afternoon."

"What?"

"It's true," Kozak insisted. "I came over when you didn't answer." Then he grinned. "But it does make a convenient excuse, doesn't it?"

Resigned, Seth took his friend up to the cabin. Kozak stripped off his jacket and left it slung over the balcony rail, then the two went inside. Seth headed for the coffeepot and Kozak made a beeline for the radio.

"Who is she, anyway?" he asked. "Women of that caliber don't show up here every day. Where'd she come from? What's she doing?"

"You won't believe it," Seth said, busy in the kitchen. "She's a reporter—writes newspaper stories about movie stars. Somebody told her that a dead rock-and-roll singer was still alive. Rafer Fernando, remember him?"

"Yeah, his songs were just getting popular when I was in Nam."

"Well, she heard he was hiding up here, so she came looking. Somebody in Deer Lick gave her the impression I was him."

"Somebody in Deer Lick?"

"Yeah, crazy, right?"

"I don't know," Kozak murmured, already prying the radiophone apart with his army knife. "Those kids who broke in here last year, maybe?"

"Who knows? It's just a rumor. Anyway, the weather got bad, so she was stuck here. I was going to bring her over to your place last night, but she—we had a mishap in the lake."

"What kind of mishap?"

"She got scared swimming, came close to shock. So I kept her here another night to keep an eye."

"Hmm," said Kozak.

Seth finished measuring coffee and plugged the pot in. Then he rounded the counter and approached Kozak as he tinkered with the radio. "What's that supposed to mean?"

Kozak put down his knife and reached into the wiring with his fingers. Sounding noncommittal, he said, "Doesn't mean anything."

"Like hell it doesn't."

Silent, Kozak held up a length of wire and a small plastic plug.

"What's that?"

"What's it look like? No, forget I asked. You may be God's gift to the biochemical world, but you're an idiot when it comes to electronics. Trust me, it's important stuff. Your equipment's been disconnected."

"What?"

"You heard me. And things like this don't come apart without some help, either." Kozak looked at Seth steadily. "You pull the plug?"

"Of course not." Seth struggled with the wave of disbelief. "Why would I shut off the radio?"

Kozak shrugged. "Some people take the phone off the hook when they don't want to be disturbed in the sack—"

"Cut the funny stuff."

"Somebody disconnected your communications, that's all. This particular wire was pulled so the lights would still work—so you wouldn't notice the sound was off. Smart job, if you ask me. You didn't do it, though. So who did?"

Seth stared at the evidence Kozak dangled before his eyes. Stunned, Seth said, "I don't—I don't know."

"Your lady friend? You say she's a reporter?"

Seth tried to think, tried to imagine Catty doing such a thing. When had she done it? More importantly, why? His head had been in turmoil just minutes earlier—turmoil caused by the sweet sound of her cries, the supple twisting of her body beneath his own. Her shyness was erotic, her awkward innocence an incredible turn-on for him. Had it all been deliberate? "Yes," he said, trying to marshal his thoughts. "She's a reporter."

"And she's looking for a dead rock-and-roll singer? You're sure?"

Angry, Seth snapped, "Who would make up a story that crazy if it wasn't true?"

Kozak folded his arms, his face bland. "Somebody who was on the trail of a bigger story, I'd say. How much does she know about you, Seth? You tell her everything you've told me?"

"No," said Seth said slowly. "Not everything."

Kozak swore. "How much *did* you tell her? About your old man, for instance?"

"No, but—"

"She get you into bed to talk? She want to know about the chemicals you stole?" Kozak grabbed Seth's shoulder and shook it. "Damn it, man, *how much does she know*?"

Catty brushed her teeth and dressed herself. Her trousers and panties had dried by the fire during the night, and she was glad to get into them. The only thing that would make her happier would be Seth slowly taking her *out* of them again. She was still trembling inside. She hoped he'd get rid of Kozak quickly. With her briefcase over her shoulder, she headed for the cabin to join the men.

But she happened to glance down at the dock in time to see a canoe sliding in. Sitting in the stern was the boy from Bob's Bait and Tackle shop.

He waved. "Hi, Miss Sinclair! Remember me?"

Catty dropped her briefcase and raced down to the dock to shut him up before he announced his arrival to Seth. "Shh! What do you think you're doing here?"

The boy looked astonished. "Why, I came to get you. Don't you remember? I'm the one who brought you here before the storm. I—"

"I know who you are! Go away, will you?"

"But—but—I thought—"

"Look, kid, don't waste your brain cells. I don't want to be rescued, get it? I've changed my mind. I'm going to stay here for a while. So paddle yourself back to—"

"You want to stay here, lady? With Mr. *Bernstein*?"

"Keep your voice down!" Catty hissed. "You want him to hear you? Scram!"

His eyes popped open. "Is he keeping you prisoner?"

"Oh, for God's sake! Just go, will you? He'll be out in a minute!"

"I heard he's dangerous, lady. My older brother Jesse and his friends used to come up here—for parties with girls, you

SILHOUETTE®

PRESENTS ♥

A Real Sweetheart of a Deal!

6 FREE GIFTS

PEEL BACK THIS CARD AND SEE WHAT YOU CAN GET! THEN...

Complete the Hand Inside ➤

It's easy! To play your cards right, just match this card with the cards inside.

Turn over for more details ...

Incredible, isn't it? Deal yourself in right now and get 6 fabulous gifts
ABSOLUTELY FREE.

1. 4 BRAND NEW SILHOUETTE DESIRE® NOVELS—FREE!
Sit back and enjoy the excitement, romance and thrills of four fantastic novels. You'll receive them as part of this winning streak!

2. A LOVELY BRACELET WATCH—FREE!

You'll love your elegant bracelet watch—this classic LCD quartz watch is a perfect expression of your style and good taste—and it's yours free as an added thanks for giving our Reader Service a try!

3. AN EXCITING MYSTERY BONUS—FREE!
And still your luck holds! You'll also receive a special mystery bonus. You'll be thrilled with this surprise gift. It will be the source of many compliments as well as a useful and attractive addition to your home.

PLUS
THERE'S MORE. THE DECK IS STACKED IN YOUR FAVOR. HERE ARE THREE MORE WINNING POINTS. YOU'LL ALSO RECEIVE:

4. FREE HOME DELIVERY
Imagine how you'll enjoy having the chance to preview the romantic adventures of our Silhouette heroines in the convenience of your own home! Here's how it works. Every month we'll deliver 6 new Silhouette Desire® novels right to your door. There's no obligation to buy, and if you decide to keep them, they'll be yours for only $2.24* each—that's a savings of 26¢ per book! And there's no charge for postage and handling—there are no hidden extras!

5. A MONTHLY NEWSLETTER—FREE!
It's our special "Silhouette" Newsletter—our members' privileged look at upcoming books and profiles of our most popular authors.

6. MORE GIFTS FROM TIME TO TIME—FREE!
It's easy to see why you have the winning hand. In addition to all the other special deals available only to our home subscribers, when you join the Silhouette Reader Service, you can look forward to additional free gifts throughout the year.

SO DEAL YOURSELF IN—YOU CAN'T HELP BUT WIN!
*In the future, prices and terms may change, but you always have the opportunity to cancel your subscription. Sales taxes applicable in N.Y. and Iowa.

You'll Fall In Love With This Sweetheart Deal From Silhouette!

SILHOUETTE READER SERVICE™
FREE OFFER CARD

4 FREE BOOKS • FREE BRACELET WATCH
• FREE MYSTERY BONUS • FREE HOME DELIVERY
• INSIDER'S NEWSLETTER • MORE SURPRISE
GIFTS

YES! Deal me in. Please send me four free Silhouette Desire novels, the bracelet watch and my free mystery bonus as explained on the opposite page. If I'm not fully satisfied I can cancel at any time, but if I choose to continue in the Reader Service I'll pay the low members-only price each month.

225 CIS JAY2
(U-S-D-09/89)

First Name   Last Name

PLEASE PRINT

Address   Apt.

City   State   Zip Code

Offer limited to one per household and not valid to current Silhouette Desire subscribers. All orders subject to approval.

SILHOUETTE NO RISK GUARANTEE

- There is no obligation to buy—the free books and gifts remain yours to keep.
- You'll receive books before they're available in stores.
- You may end your subscription at any time—by sending us a note or a shipping statement marked "cancel" or by returning any unopened shipment to us by parcel post at our expense.

PRINTED IN U.S.A.

Remember! To win this hand, all you have to do is place your sticker inside and DETACH AND MAIL THE CARD BELOW. You'll get four free books, a free bracelet watch and a mystery bonus.
BUT DON'T DELAY!
MAIL US YOUR LUCKY CARD TODAY!

If card is missing write to:
Silhouette Reader Service, 901 Fuhrmann Blvd., P.O. Box 1867, Buffalo, N.Y. 14269-1867

BUSINESS REPLY CARD

First Class   Permit No. 717   Buffalo, NY

Postage will be paid by addressee

SILHOUETTE READER SERVICE™
901 Fuhrmann Blvd.
P.O. Box 1867
Buffalo, N.Y.
14240-9952

NO POSTAGE
NECESSARY
IF MAILED
IN THE
UNITED STATES

know? Only Bernstein chased them away. He's got a gun and wild dogs and—why, my brother got buckshot in his—"

Catty controlled her urge to scream. She snatched up a rock and reared back as if to hurl it at the boy. "Will you shut up? Mr. Bernstein is not dangerous. Tell Jesse to take his girlfriends elsewhere! Now, get *out* of here, will you? I—no, wait!"

The boy nearly dropped his paddle, but he stopped trying to splash his way out of her rock-throwing range. "Yes?"

Catty was thinking fast. Things had changed. She wasn't sure why, but suddenly she wasn't thinking of herself anymore—nor about the story she had been so hungry for just hours earlier. No, now she had another cause in mind. Possibly, there was something she could do for Seth.

She looked at the kid and asked, "Could you take a letter for me?"

"Huh?"

"If I write a letter would you take it to the nearest post office for me? I'd pay you. I'll make it worth your while."

The kid said, "I live right beside the Deer Lick post office."

"Wonderful," Catty breathed. "Wait right here."

She ran back up the path and grabbed her briefcase. Inside, she found her notebook and a pen. She scribbled a quick note to her part-time assistant, a young woman who also free-lanced in the library department at the New York newspaper.

Sharon: Need info on a Seth Barnhurst. Top secret. Reply ASAP care of Deer Lick post office.

Catty.

Maybe there was something Sharon could dig up that could help Seth's situation. She laughed once and shook her head. It was true she was curious and there was no telling when Seth would say more, but she was certain she'd be able to help once she got things figured out, and she simply couldn't sit still twiddling her thumbs until he opened up. She had to do something. For once, here she was, doing something noble. Catty Sinclair, of all people!

She folded the note and crammed it into the only envelope she had in the briefcase—a used one. She had some money in the case, but not enough to pay for express delivery and buy the kid's services, too. Her wallet was in her jacket pocket in the cabin.

She started up the path toward the porch but stopped on the cabin steps, realizing she'd have to alert Seth to the boy's arrival if she went inside. Crouched beneath a window, she could hear Seth and Kozak talking inside, and she didn't want Seth to know she had yet another offer of transportation back home.

Then her eyes fell upon Mike Kozak's jacket left on the balcony railing. "Perfect," she whispered. "Now, let's hope Kozak brought cash."

She sneaked onto the porch and lifted the jacket. Silently, she rifled the pockets. All was fair if you got what you wanted—that had always been Catty's motto. Triumph! He kept a leather billfold in the inside pocket and Catty found a ten-dollar bill and a couple of singles. But something stopped her.

"Good Lord," she muttered. "What's wrong with me?"

She stared at the wallet for a moment, then noticed something tucked between the dollar bills. With thumb and forefinger, Catty lifted out the object. It was a neat, square, foil-wrapped package—the kind of thing you were supposed to find in a man's wallet.

With a grin, Catty tucked it into her trouser pocket. She couldn't take the money, but this was another matter altogether.

She put the wallet back and left the jacket exactly the way she'd found it, then hurried back to the kid.

"Will you take this bracelet?"

"Huh?" The boy looked disgusted. "A bracelet? What for?"

"It's all I've got at the moment. Look, it's a nice bracelet. I love it dearly. My sister gave it to me. I want it back, of course. You keep it until I see you again, then I promise I'll pay you double what everything costs you."

"Gee, I don't know..."

"It's solid gold!" Catty cried. "And it's engraved, see? 'From Nina with love.' Now doesn't that prove something? Look, damn your eyes, this is the most important piece of jewelry I own. If you lose it, I'll murder you. Just consider it collateral, will you? I need—"

"You're making me feel like a jerk," said the kid. "If it's that important, I'll do it for free."

"Free?" Catty exclaimed.

"You can pay me back," he said quickly. "I trust you."

Surprised but thankful, Catty gave the boy directions on how to send the message to Sharon and return to the island as soon as he heard an answer. Then Catty hustled him away as soon as the deal was struck.

Seth and Kozak left the cabin together. Seth felt furious, but he was sure Kozak's cooler head had planned a better strategy.

"You understand?" Kozak asked. "I'll come back tomorrow to pick her up, after I've delivered supplies up to the Marchand cabin. "I'll stop back this evening. In the meantime, you find out what she's up to."

"I will."

"Before it's too late," Kozak added. He picked up his jacket from the railing and slung it over his shoulder. "I'll do anything I can to help. Just remember—I'm a law-abiding man, so I won't help you bury that pretty body if you murder her."

In no mood for jokes, Seth said curtly, "I'll keep that in mind."

Catty was coming up the path from the lake, and she smiled when she saw the men standing on the porch. "You two have a nice chat?"

"Sure," Kozak said. "I was telling Seth about the bear I saw this morning."

"A bear?" Catty looked startled.

"Yeah, swimming in the lake. We had a rogue male around here last year. Maybe it's him again. I didn't get close enough for a good look."

"Understandable."

He smiled. "Yeah. Look, I've got to be running along. I spoke with Seth about transporting you, Miss Sinclair. I've got a run to make today, but I'll be back tonight. In the morning, I'll be glad to take you anywhere you have to go. Did you leave a rental car in Deer Lick?"

Seth saw Catty's expression tighten. She didn't want to leave the island yet, and that wish was apparent in her face. She said, "No, I don't drive. I took a bus to Deer Lick."

"Buses leave every day from there."

"Oh," she said. "Wonderful. I—uh—my story didn't pan out, so I guess there's no sense hanging around."

"Tomorrow, then. If you want to leave sooner than that, Seth will have to take you in his boat."

Catty looked relieved. "Oh, I'll wait."

She tipped her head and smiled at Seth. He didn't respond. He didn't plan on encouraging the little witch any more. Catty must have seen his look, because her ingenuous smile faltered.

"Okay," Kozak said. "It's all set. If you need anything sooner, just call on the radiophone." Casually, he added, "I just fixed it. Did you happen to notice it was broken?"

Catty blinked. With a perfectly innocent expression on her face, she said, "Me? I don't know beans about radios."

"Hmm," said Kozak, starting down the steps. "Well, it's fixed now. Goodbye, Miss Sinclair. It was great meeting you. Keep your eyes open for bears."

Seth accompanied Kozak to the dock and helped him untie the Queen Victoria. Kozak shook Seth's hand and gave him some good advice. "Be careful," he said.

Seth watched Kozak pull the boat out onto the lake and rev the powerful engines. They waved. A moment later, Seth heard Catty on the dock beside him. He didn't turn around, but he felt her touch him. She put her hands on his back, and as Kozak's boat pulled into the distance, she slid her arms around Seth's waist. Her body felt warm and willing against his. Her breasts fit nicely into the curve of his lower back. His own body began to betray him. Although his mind was shouting, the parts of his anatomy that he couldn't control responded to her nearness.

"I like Kozak," she said, her voice quietly intimate in his ear. "He seems like a nice man."

Stiffly, Seth said, "He's my good friend."

"Do you have many other friends? Around here, I mean?"

Seth turned in her embrace then. She clung to him, and he put his hands on her shoulders. He must have grabbed her hard, because her brown eyes suddenly widened. Seth did not loosen his hold. He was only conscious of the anger inside, anger that was seething to get out.

"Why?" he demanded. "Why do you want to know?"

Catty stared up at him, startled by the violent undercurrent in his voice. "I—I just wondered, that's all. What's wrong?"

"You ask a hell of a lot of questions."

"I thought we were getting to know each other."

"Is that what you planned from the start?"

"What are you talking about? I didn't plan anything—"

He tightened his grip, hands biting into her flesh. "Has all of it been an act, Catty?"

"What?"

"Starting from the first day, tell me the truth. Did you really come here looking for Rafer Fernando?"

Catty looked mystified. "What happened between you and Kozak? What the hell did he tell you about me?"

"He didn't tell me a damn thing. Except that the radio had been sabotaged."

"You don't think *I*—"

"There are only two of us, Catty, and I sure as hell didn't pull any wires."

"I don't know what you're talking about!"

She put on a good act, but Seth knew her well enough to see that it was all bluster. Furious and half afraid he couldn't stop himself from hurting her, he turned Catty loose, spinning her around so hard she stumbled. But she whirled around to face him, a fighter to the end.

Seth said, "The radio was dead. Did you do it?"

Her face turned bright pink, but her courage didn't flag. "All right, yes! Yes, I did sabotage your stupid radio. But—"

"Why?"

"Because I— Oh, hell, I don't know." Seth took a pace toward her. Catty backed up the path and nearly fell, but she caught her balance on a tree limb. "I thought it was obvious. I felt good with you. I wanted—for crying out loud,

Kozak was going to come for me last night, and I wanted a few more hours, that's all.''

"What for?"

"Because I— What's *wrong* with you? I thought we hit it off! I thought—"

"What do you want from me, Catty? It's all been an act, hasn't it? The charming scene in the lake? Damn, you had me going! Last night, too? And this morning when you played the frightened virgin and told me the sob story—"

The wounded expression on her face lasted less than one second. Then Catty stopped on the path and stood up to him at last, her eyes flashing, her whole body trembling. "It was not a sob story!"

Seth grabbed her again, his grip biting into the flesh of her forearm. "Don't lie to me, Catty. Damn you, don't lie."

She didn't flinch. Through gritted teeth, she said, "I'm not lying. I told you things I've never told anyone in my life. If it didn't sound natural, forgive me. I'm not used to revealing my deepest secrets."

"Secrets!" Seth said disparagingly. "The only kind of secrets you know are the ones that make good headlines." He pushed Catty off the path and shoved her against the nearest tree trunk. She didn't cry out, but he could see she had to bite down to stop herself. He held one wrist behind her back and used his body to pin her slight frame against the tree. She squirmed, then gasped when he stopped her by jamming his knee between her legs. He could feel her heart hammering against his own chest, the heat of her fear.

"Tell me a few more secrets now, Catty," he rasped, his mouth next to her ear. "The truth this time. You're not really the little innocent you've been pretending to be, are you? You got me into bed and expected me to spill my guts, didn't you?"

"No!"

"That pathetic story you told me about your sister—"

"That was the truth!"

"Well, you're just like her, aren't you? Only you get paid in information. You're a different kind of whore."

Catty yanked one hand free and slapped him. She didn't stop there, either. With Seth off balance, she kicked her way free, then spun around on the path and faced him with all the fury of a cornered bobcat.

"Shut up," she seethed, tears of rage trembling in her fiery eyes. "Just shut up and listen. Everything I've told you is true. I came here looking for a story, and when you didn't turn out to be Rafer, I thought I had another story right in the palm of my hand. But something happened. It doesn't happen all the time, either. I started to *like* you!"

"Don't—"

"I decided *not* to write about you, dammit. I wanted to spend more time with you! Yes, I messed up the radio because I—damn, I just thought we'd have another day together. You idiot, don't you see?"

"Explain it to me!"

"You made me feel like a person!" The words burst from her. Catty's face froze then. Obviously, she wanted to snatch back the statement.

Seth turned away. He felt sick—of all of it. He said, "I don't believe you."

"I'm not surprised," she snapped, behind him. "Trusting is not your strong suit."

Seth swung around and glowered at her. "You haven't given me much reason to trust."

Catty stood straight as a ramrod, but quivered with anger. "Don't blame me. You don't want to believe anyone but yourself."

"You don't know anything about me."

"It doesn't take a genius to see that you're not exactly running from anything, Doctor! You're hiding!"

"You don't know what you're talking about!"

"Don't I? You *like* it out here in never-never land, don't you? There's nobody to deal with, nobody to force you into believing in anything but yourself. Except for Kozak, and he's safe because he's just as much of a hermit as you are! You trust him because you know he'll never leave this god-forsaken place."

Seth didn't expect her to understand. She didn't know what he'd been through, the choices he'd made to protect a great many people. Shortly, Seth said, "I don't need anyone to keep my secrets for me."

"It's not just secrets you're keeping," Catty said. "It's emotion. You've locked yourself away nice and tight, but I've stumbled into your sanctuary and made a mess of things."

"You're damned right!"

"That's what happens when you start living in the real world, Seth. Right now, you're in a vacuum—a nice, safe vacuum. All your garbage about self-examination and looking inside yourself—it's all because you haven't got anyone to share your life with, isn't it?"

"I don't need anyone. I don't want anyone."

"Because you're scared," Catty said bluntly and jammed her finger into his chest to make her point. "Admit it. You're scared of me, buster. Not just of what I could write about you, but of *me*—a woman who has gotten under your skin."

Six

With that, Catty stormed off the path and headed into the woods, clearly wanting to be alone.

Seth stayed where he was, emotion roiling hard inside him. He shouted after her. "Where are you going?"

"None of your business!"

"Come back here!"

"Make me!" she bellowed over her shoulder.

"Catty," he shouted, "running away isn't your style!"

"I'm only giving you what *you* want!"

"It isn't safe. There's probably a bear wandering around here. If you get yourself eaten, I'll be—"

On a rock above him, she spun around in a flurry of sun-splashed hair. Fire blazed in her eyes as she glared at him. "You'll be what? Mildly distressed?"

"Enormously relieved," he snapped. "But I'll probably feel guilty, too."

"Well, I'd *hate* to make you feel guilty," Catty cracked.

Seth climbed the rocks to reach her, then found he couldn't close the final few yards between them. He wasn't sure he could keep his hands off her slender neck. How could one woman make him think so often of violence? With difficulty, he choked out the next words. "Don't go wandering around. You might get hurt."

"Oh, *really*? A minute ago you were manhandling me like King Kong! Why worry about violating your Hippocritic oath now?"

"That's Hippocratic," Seth ground out. "Damn your eyes, you make me crazy!"

"Forgive me," she retorted mercilessly. "I didn't mean to squeeze any remotely human response out of you!"

That did it. In a single leap, he reached her. Catty froze, stubbornly refusing to be intimidated. Her wall of defense was clearly in place now, but—fed up and furious—Seth drove his fingers into her hair, forcing Catty's face up to his. Close enough to kiss her, he said, "You have no right to come barging into my life like this."

She tightened her chin and glared. "Believe me, I can't wait to get off this island! But I'm stuck until Kozak gets back. Take your hands off me."

"Why? Are you suddenly scared? You're afraid of me, too, aren't you?"

"Bull."

"Yes, you are. In the same kind of way."

"Lay off. I'm happy with my life. I've got friends and a good living. I haven't cut myself off from society."

"Not physically," Seth said. "But you keep an unbreakable lock on your heart, Catty."

"Do us both a favor," she rejoined furiously. "Cut with the amateur psychoanalyzing. You want privacy? Fine, I'll give it to you. I'll spend the day on the other side of the island. Now let me go before I kick you where it'll do the most damage."

The icy look in her eye showed she meant every word. Seth loosened his grip and released her. "Much as I'd like you to disappear," he snapped, "I can't let you wander off with a dangerous animal on the loose. That bear is probably looking for a place to hibernate and wouldn't turn down a last meal—even one as bitter as you."

Catty's temper blazed. "I hope he doesn't have the gall to try hibernating *here* this winter! To think—you might actually have to exist with another living creature for several months!"

"Oh, shut up."

"With pleasure."

"There are times," he said, "when I'd like to sock you."

"Go ahead, Barnhurst." Catty thrust her face at him, her eyes burning. "If it makes you feel better, I can take it."

Seth recoiled from her. "I don't want to hit you."

"Sure you do. It's easy." Her eyes were on fire. "It's certainly easier than dealing with everything else inside, isn't it?"

She was right about that. He did want to settle things— but violence wasn't going to solve anything. Seth tried to jam a lid on everything else and think.

An indomitable energy burned inside this woman, a flame so bright that Seth could understand why some men might feel intimidated by it and lash out. It was her will to live, her desire to make something of herself, but it masqueraded as arrogance. She had raised insolence to an art form. And the dangerous gleam in her eye could be mistaken for disdain, too.

But the tiny tremor at the corner of her mouth gave Catty away. She could put on a good front at the drop of a hat, but inside she was quaking. Only someone who understood how her mind worked could notice that she was shivering ever so slightly with her pent-up emotion—the same way she had shivered with desire just two hours earlier. All passion boiled close to the surface with Catty.

The moment seemed to stretch for her, too. Catty glared back at him for several heartbeats—her cheeks bright, her hands trembling.

Seth said, "I don't want to hurt you, Catty."

"Good! Because I'd face a bear single-handed before I'd let you touch me."

She turned and left him then, striding rapidly for the cabin, a virago in miniature, a furious goddess in high-heeled boots. She gained the porch and threw open the cabin door. It banged on its hinges so hard the cabin seemed to shake on its foundation. Without a backward look, Catty marched through.

Seth felt shaken—sick inside. He put his hand against a tree branch and leaned there, waiting for his stomach to settle, his heartbeat to slow down. He needed time to examine things, to figure out what was going on.

But Catty wasn't going to give him time. He could hear her slamming around in the cabin. Slowly, he followed her, half afraid to confront her again, but inexplicably drawn.

When he opened the door of the cabin, Seth stopped dead. He saw Catty clumsily trying to yank one of his guns down off the rack over the mantel.

With a curse, Seth flung himself across the room. "Don't be insane, woman!"

Before he reached her, she managed to heave the heavy gun off its rack and staggered backward, unbalanced by the weight of the weapon.

"Catty, stop! That's a loaded gun!"

"I know it's loaded! I'm not stupid!" She jammed the barrel under her arm, then broke open the stock for safety's sake and checked the shells. Triumphantly, she glared at him. "I know what I'm doing. So stay away from me."

The dogs were delighted by the appearance of the gun. Shooting sports, they knew, always involved them. They began to leap around Catty, whining in excitement. Their fickleness was the last straw. Anger renewed, Seth asked, "What are you planning to do with that? Take potshots at me now?"

"Sounds tempting," she snapped, attempting to cut around him, "But no—I won't spend another minute with you. I'm leaving."

"Where are you going?"

"I'll spend the day on the other side of the island. If I run into any trouble, I'll have this to protect myself."

Seth blocked her exit. "You'll do no such thing—not with a loaded shotgun. There'll be some kind of accident."

"I've handled guns before. I did a story about a shooting range and I learned exactly how to handle firearms."

"That's not a handgun."

"I know what it is!" Sarcastically, she said, "But obviously, you don't believe a word I say, so why should I bother trying to convince you otherwise?"

Seth bit down on his anger. "A shotgun won't stop a bear, you know. It'll only make him mad."

"What'll it do to a human being?" she demanded.

"Are you threatening me?"

"Only if you don't get out of my way!"

Seth had no choice but to stand aside. The dogs scrambled after Catty ecstatically. Seth tailed them outside again, following the absurd figure Catty made—a hot-blooded blonde toting a shotgun almost as big as she was. He wanted to stop her, but she obviously knew enough about guns to handle it correctly. She clattered down the porch steps, heading for the woods. She actually intended to spend the day sitting on a rock waiting for Kozak!

"Catty," Seth called.

She disappeared into the trees and brush. Seth sighed. To himself, he growled, "Unbelievable."

He fumed about her for half a minute, torn between reason and instinct. His brain shouted one clear message—to let her do what she wanted—but his gut had a different story. Then common sense prevailed and he followed her. But halfway into the first bank of bushes, Seth heard one of the dogs start to yelp. And then Catty cried out.

In fact, Catty screamed.

Seth rocketed through the underbrush.

Catty screamed and screamed, both dogs began to bark and howl, and the next sound Seth heard was the unmistakable growling roar of a bear.

What happened next took place in less than fifteen seconds, but all the action seemed to grind in excruciatingly slow motion. Seth crashed through the bushes, heading for the sound of Catty's voice. She came barreling backward with one dog underfoot so that all three of them collided in a tangle of thorny bushes and blinding tree branches. Seth felt the swat of pine needles rake across his eyes, then he opened his arms and caught Catty, her momentum driving them both into the nearest tree. Seth managed to stand and whirl Catty behind him. Then he turned and saw the bear.

It was a big animal, all muscle and slashing teeth. Reared back on its hind legs and pawing the air with its foreclaws, it thundered toward Sam, who was barking like crazy in the bear's path, willing to defend them to the death.

"Look out!" Catty cried.

Seth wasn't sure what he intended to do. He stood between Catty and the bear, but she darted sideways. In the next instant, he saw her put the shotgun unsteadily to her shoulder.

"Catty, *wait*!" he cried, stepping forward.

But she pulled the trigger at exactly the same moment the dog crashed against her legs. The gun exploded with a tremendous noise. Catty tumbled backward from the recoil of both barrels discharging at once, Sam yelped, the bear froze for an excruciating second. Seth was spun around like a top, and fell.

Then the pain hit him like a runaway train.

As soon as she fired the gun, Catty knew she'd made a dreadful mistake. The bear fled as she'd planned, but the dog leapt into the air and collapsed in a writhing heap. Seth just whirled around and dropped. Choking with fear, Catty threw down the gun and ran to him.

"Seth! Oh, my God!"

She rocked to a stop, horrified. Sprawled face down across the weeds and stone, Seth looked limp—his arms and legs cast wide, his head twisted between two stones. Catty stumbled over the brush and threw herself down by his side. He didn't move. She hugged herself, afraid to touch him, afraid to see if he was breathing. Tears of panic clogged her throat and blinded her eyes. Though she hadn't prayed in years, Catty began to beg for his life.

"Please, please," she whispered.

At last, with hands shaking, she reached and took hold of Seth's shoulders. Weeping, she struggled to roll him over, then caught her breath at the sight of him. Seth's face was pale, except for an ugly bruise on his forehead that was welling with blood. His shirt was dotted with blood, too, and his right sleeve was soaked with it. Seeing the stains, Catty gasped out a sob.

But the sight of it galvanized her into action. She leapt to her feet, suddenly terrified that the bear was on his way back. Taking Seth by his good arm, she tried to drag him toward the cabin, but the ground was too rough. She only managed to tug him a few yards before he made a noise. Catty threw herself down beside him and gathered him into her arms. He stirred groggily, and finally cursed.

"Dear God," Catty pleaded. "Please don't let him die. Oh, Seth!" Maybe she cradled him too hard for Seth groaned and woke, pushing weakly out of her embrace.

"Seth! I'm so sorry! I only meant to frighten it away, not—"

"Take it easy," he said thickly. Gingerly, he put his hand to his forehead.

Catty hiccuped and cried, holding him tightly. "Tell me what to do! Oh, God. You're hurt, you're—"

"Damn," he muttered, blinking. "What the hell did you do that for?"

"I didn't mean to shoot you. It was the bear!"

He felt his shoulder and bit down on an exclamation. He squeezed his eyes closed as if to hold in the pain.

"Quick," Catty said, climbing to her knees. "We've got to get you inside. The bear might come back any second."

"You scared it too badly. It won't come back." Seth spoke carefully—like a man who'd had too much to drink. He blinked and tried to focus his eyes. "Wow. What a headache."

"You're bleeding—your shoulder. What can I do?"

That woke him up. "Press something on it. Use your hand—anything."

She obeyed. Seth gasped again, and Catty whimpered, hating the idea of hurting him more than he was already.

Grinding his back teeth, Seth said, "How bad is my chest?"

With her other hand, Catty unbuttoned his shirt and pushed it aside. Her own vision was so blurry she could hardly see. "I—I can't tell. There's blood, but—"

"Is it flowing?"

"Not like your shoulder. Oh, Seth—"

"Take it easy. I'm not going to die. I'm just full of buck-shot."

Catty choked and began to cry for real. She covered her face with her blood-smeared hand.

Seth shuddered on a laugh. "What's this? A few minutes ago we were talking about doing real damage to each other and now you're squeamish!"

"Don't joke," Catty wept. "Not about this. I could have killed you."

"I'm not out of my misery yet. Can you help me stand up? I seem to be a little on the weak side."

Awkwardly, Catty slid her arm beneath his back and assisted Seth into an upright position. They tussled for a moment, but Seth managed to sway to his feet. He nearly passed out, sweat breaking out on his face, and Catty staggered under his weight, but she knew she had to get him to shelter. Fiercely determined, she guided him down the hillside, struggling to keep him from falling on his face.

"Wait," he said once, and stood for a second trying to clear his head.

"Just a few more steps," Catty begged.

They reached the porch at last. With difficulty, Catty guided him into one of the chairs.

"Get me a couple of towels," Seth said, closing his eyes and trying to catch his breath. He pressed his hand against his forehead, wincing once. "And some ice. There's also some first-aid stuff in a black bag under the sink."

He looked terribly pale and sick, but Catty had no choice but to leave him alone for a few seconds. She found everything he asked for and returned to the porch, cradling towels, the bag and two trays of ice cubes. But when she saw Seth in the chair, his head thrown back loosely, his arm dripping blood onto the porch floor, she felt every nerve in her body tighten with fear.

But he opened his eyes groggily. "Steady," he mumbled. "I'm okay."

She knelt beside him. "I thought— Oh, Seth."

He managed a grin. "Towel, please. Let's fill it with ice."

He tried to do the job, but from weakness or shock, he was too clumsy to manage by himself. Catty took the towel back. "Here, let me."

She snapped some ice cubes into one of the towels and handed it to Seth, who held the makeshift icepack against his forehead. Then Catty pressed the other towel against his shoulder for a minute, not speaking. With the back of her hand, she skimmed the tears from her eyes. "I—I shot Sam, too."

Seth said, "He looks healthy enough to me."

Catty jerked her attention to the edge of the porch where the two dogs were crouched, nervously watching. Sam did indeed look alive and relatively well. His black coat was dotted with the same spray of pellet wounds that Seth suffered, but the dog saw Catty's face turn toward him and began to wag his tail. Catty gave a sigh of relief and that was all the signal the dogs needed. They dashed to her side and began licking her face and Seth's.

Laughing a little, Catty shoved them away, then steeled herself to peek under the towel. Only an ooze of fresh blood seeped up from the torn patch of flesh. She could see that a bundle of shotgun pellets had penetrated the fleshy part of his upper arm and ripped through, creating a larger exit wound through which most of the blood escaped.

Seth craned his head and peered at the wound, too. "It may have nicked the artery," he said. "We'll know in a few minutes."

"Dear Lord. You might bleed to death?"

"Think positively," Seth coached, looking at her from under the crude ice pack. "It's the first rule of medicine."

"What should I do? If your artery is—"

"Just keep up the pressure a little longer."

She did, then unbuttoned his shirt and used the edge of the towel to sop up the worst of the blood from his chest.

Biting her lips, she examined the small wounds. She could see the buckshot pellets embedded in his skin.

"Think you can take those out?" Seth asked, noticing the direction of her attention.

"Shouldn't we wait for someone else? Kozak, maybe?"

"Hell, I don't want *him* poking around with a set of sharp tweezers!"

"You won't want me to do it, either."

Seth put out his hand and slid his hands into her hair. "You're not such a bad nurse," he said.

"I create my own patients!"

"Don't be so hard on yourself. It was an accident."

"It was stupid. I let myself get out of control. I'm no better than my—than anyone."

"You were going to say your father."

Catty couldn't meet his eye. "I—I went a little crazy. I hate myself when I do things like that."

Seth managed to look amused. "You shoot people often?"

"No! But—I don't know. I get out of control sometimes."

"We all do."

"You don't."

"I didn't think I did," he murmured. "Until I met you."

"I'm sorry," Catty said hastily. "I shouldn't have said the things I did earlier. I provoked you."

"You spoke the truth."

"For once."

He cocked a look at her.

Catty felt herself blushing. "I'm not always honest, I know that. I'm sorry. But—you made me so angry."

Seth sighed and shifted the ice on his forehead. "It's not just anger that gets us so worked up. It's a lot of intense emotions. They just get confused—stirred up into one gigantic storm. Pride and fear. Emotions are tough to handle. Even love.''

She laughed shortly. "No, not love. Love can't have anything to do with the kind of anger I've seen."

Seth fell silent for a moment. Then he said, "Your father again."

"Yeah, he used to get furious. I mean—there was murder in his eyes sometimes. That was never connected with love."

"I think it was in a way. He was protecting you—or he thought he was."

Shaking her head, Catty said, "He never loved me."

"What's not to love about you?"

She tried to grin. "I'll bet you could name a few of my least likable qualities right now."

"Along with a few of your best." Seth hesitated. Then his hand touched her face, brushing her cheek to remove a tear. His eyes looked smoky and troubled. He said, "Catty, I shouldn't have spoken to you the way I did."

"About the radio? Sure, you should have. You were right. I was being a jerk. I don't deserve to be trusted. But I— Look, I want you to know that I—I wouldn't write about you, Seth. That's the truth."

"I think it is," he murmured. Then his fingertips traced the line of her jaw, and his hand magically slipped around to the back of her neck. He hesitated, then gently pulled Catty's head closer until their lips were almost touching. Seth said, "But you didn't have to shoot me to make me believe you."

He kissed her. It was gentle and altogether too brief. No doubt he meant it to buck her up, but Catty felt anything but composed when she sat back on her heels.

Seth grinned at her expression. "Feel better?"

"N-no. But my state of health isn't the issue." She pulled herself together. "We'd better get you fixed up. Tell me what to do."

"Let's have a look at the arm first. Ah, see? Bleeding's stopped."

Catty took a cautious peek at the wound. "Are you blind? It's a mess!"

"That's old stuff. No new bleeding. The artery must be intact. We'll just clean this up, bandage it and see how things go. Right now, I'm not up to sewing myself. Unless you'd like to try?"

"Listen," Catty confided, "I send my clothes to the tailor if I pop a button. If you think it won't get worse, you're better off without me stabbing around with a needle."

"Candor is appreciated," Seth said. And he asked for some water and antiseptic. With his help, Catty managed to bandage his arm. He only jerked once under her ministrations, and Catty carefully finished taping.

"Not bad," he said when the job was done. "Now, the tough part. Unless these pellets come out, I'm a good candidate for a case of blood poisoning." He was already shivering and sweating at the same time, Catty could see, though she hadn't the faintest idea what that meant. With one hand, he rummaged in the bag for the right equipment and finally gave several items to Catty. "Go put a pot of water on the stove and get it boiling. Put these forceps in and—"

"This is sounding like major surgery!"

"Don't panic. We just need to sterilize a few things."

"Maybe we'd better call a professional."

"No," said Seth.

"Why not? For heaven's sake, you said yourself that you could get blood poisoning! What if you pass out? I'm not a doctor! I can't possibly—"

"I'll be okay," Seth insisted. "I don't want to go to a hospital."

"Because you think you'll be recognized?" Catty demanded. "Or are you worried somebody will put you under sodium Pentothal and make you tell all your secrets?"

"Of course not! I can't—I just don't want any more people to know where I am, that's all. Please, Catty." He caught her hand with his good one and held tight. "Please," he said again. "I need your help."

Catty frowned at him, and more protests were on the tip of her tongue. But she knew she had never heard such words from Seth before and it was likely she'd never hear them again. He didn't trust anyone lightly. She could see how tough it was for him to ask for her help. Catty hesitated, torn between what she knew was the wisest choice and what her heart told her she should do.

At last, she nodded. "Okay," she said. "Tell me what to do."

He talked her through the whole ordeal—from boiling the forceps and picking out each pellet one by one, to daubing each little wound with an antiseptic that made him yelp a time or two. She even managed to fill a syringe for him, but she couldn't watch when Seth injected himself in the thigh.

"You look exhausted," she said when he finally relaxed into the blanket she'd wrapped around his shoulders.

"I'm okay."

"You're beat," she said. "Come on, I'll help you up to bed."

"No."

"Yes, dammit! Come on!"

"I don't want to climb the steps."

Catty chewed her lower lip. He was looking pretty shaky, and if she dropped him going up the steps to the loft, she'd feel even more terrible.

"Okay," she said finally. "I'll make you a place to rest by the fire. A short nap, that ought to help."

He nodded, too tired to argue any further. When Catty finished inside, he went without protest and allowed her to tuck him into more blankets and a few pillows. He was asleep in minutes.

Catty spent the rest of the day in turmoil. She tried to keep busy—she did her best to tend to Sam's wounds, but soon realized she was going to need Kozak's help to finish that job properly. She made some sandwiches, then didn't have the stomach to eat. From time to time she checked on Seth, but he slept soundly for several hours.

At long last, Catty heard the purr of a boat's engine on the lake. With relief, she ran onto the porch. She thought she'd never be happier to see another human being as she was when she spotted Mike Kozak climbing out onto the dock.

She ran down the path to him. Mike was slinging a string of fish over his shoulder when she flew into view.

"Evening, Miss Sinclair!" he called when he caught sight of Catty. "I'm inviting myself for dinner."

"Never mind that," Catty said. "Seth's hurt."

All the good cheer left his expression at once. "What happened?"

She'd managed to hang onto her self-control all day when she was alone, but suddenly Catty was babbling—not making sense, but powerless to stop herself. "There was a bear, the one you told us about, and we argued and I told him I wasn't going to wait for—"

"You argued with a bear? Now, calm down a second, will you? Take a deep breath."

"You don't *understand*," Catty cried. "I shot him!"

"The bear?"

"Seth!"

Mike dropped his hand from around her neck. His eyes bulged. "You—you're crazy! My God, I never should have left him alone with you!"

"Left *him* alone? What about me? That bear was as big as—"

"I thought you said you didn't shoot the bear?"

"I was trying to scare him off, but I—well, I might have hit him, too. After all, those stupid pellets go everywhere!"

Kozak growled with frustration. "Did you shoot Seth or not?"

"It was an accident! For God's sake, you don't think I *meant* to—"

"Is he— How bad is he?"

"He's okay. He's been sleeping."

Kozak spun around and ran up the path. With Catty hot on his heels, he quickly arrived at the porch and threw open the door. He was halfway across the room before Catty caught his arm and dug in her heels. He swung around like an angry bull.

"Don't wake him," Catty commanded in a fierce whisper.

"I've got to make sure—"

"He's alive. You can see that from here. Calm down, will you? Come on, I've made some coffee."

Kozak shook off her hand, then belligerently went to stand over Seth's prone form. He stayed quiet, though, and didn't try to rouse his friend. At last, he seemed satisfied and turned around. He followed Catty to the kitchen where she poured coffee. She jerked her head toward the door, and they carried their cups onto the porch and spoke in low voices as dusk began to fall.

Catty leaned against the balcony, cupping her hands around the hot drink. "Seth told me about the radio and your suspicions. You probably hate me right now. But I—well, I'm glad you're here."

Kozak grunted and took a sip. "I don't hate you."

"You don't trust me either."

He shrugged. "Don't expect miracles."

"Look, you've got to believe that I didn't mean to hurt him. What choice did I have? The bear was going to eat Sam and the rest of us right in front of my eyes! I just didn't realize how the pellets spray out of a shotgun."

"What were you doing with the gun in the first place?"

"What?"

Kozak's eyes were narrow. "You heard me."

"It—I was going to wait for you on the other side of the island. Seth and I—we had an argument, and I wanted to leave. You weren't coming until later, so I—"

Kozak nodded. "Okay, I can fill in the rest of it. Why didn't you go to the hospital? Was he too badly hurt to run the boat?"

"He didn't want to go."

"And you?" Kozak asked.

Startled by that, Catty said, "I—I don't know the way."

Kozak didn't answer, but drank a long swallow from his cup and studied the lake as darkness grew on the water. "Well," he said, "we'd better wake up Seth before it gets pitch black out there."

"Why?"

Kozak put down his mug. "I'm taking him to the hospital, of course. I can fly him out myself."

"I think Seth will have something to say about that."

Kozak sent her a grin. "Yeah, but I'm stronger than he is."

Catty stood her ground. "You might have both of us to fight if you plan to use force."

"Oho," said Kozak, his grin fading. "I should have guessed."

"I don't know what you mean by that. Seth doesn't want to go. If that's the way he feels, I'm here to see his wishes are respected."

"You're going to stand in my way?"

"Yes, absolutely."

Kozak smiled thinly. "That figures, too."

Catty bristled. "What's that supposed to mean?"

"You tell me," Kozak coached, lazily folding his arms over his burly chest. "It must be damn convenient—keeping him captive out here. Do you think you'll get your story before he dies?"

Catty eyed Kozak coldly. "He's not going to die. As for the rest of it, Seth understands the truth about me—that's all that matters. I don't owe you a damn thing, Mr. Kozak."

"Maybe not. But I don't trust you, lady. Maybe you've snowed Seth into believing every word you say, but I'm a tougher customer. You're going to have to do more than take off your clothes to—"

"Shut up." Catty stood up and strode to the far end of the porch, determined to put some distance between them before she belted the man. She faced him, then, but fought to keep her temper under control. "I don't care what you believe. I don't care about you at all—except that you're supposed to be Seth's friend. Why, you know more about his problems than I do!"

"If it's a choice between living and dying—"

"It isn't. Wake him up, if you like. You'll see for yourself."

Softly, Kozak said, "You're in love with him, aren't you?"

Catty stared. "What the hell gives you that idea?"

Lifting his shoulders, Kozak said, "Call it loner's intuition. You've got it bad for him, haven't you?"

"I am not—I don't—I have no feelings one way or the other for—"

He laughed. "You can't even say the word, can you? Man, the two of you are a pair! Neither one of you wants to admit you might need some simple human companionship now and then."

"Oh, go take a flying leap!"

Her hot protest amused him. Mike Kozak eased himself down on the balcony railing and leaned there, studying her. "It's not a crime, you know. He's a nice guy. You'd be crazy not to go head over heels for him."

Catty felt her anger start to deflate. Maybe she'd been a fool to get steamed in the first place. She looked away from Kozak and grumbled, "A lot of good it would do me."

"Why do you say that?"

"Because," she burst out, "that man is more nervous than a tourist on the subway."

"He's got his reasons," Kozak said calmly.

"You mean the mess he's gotten himself into? Exactly my point. How does he expect to get out of it without some help? He has to start trusting somebody else eventually!"

Kozak looked at her oddly. "You've got it all wrong. It's not just you he's suspicious of. Seth doesn't trust himself."

That revelation surprised her.

"I've said too much," Kozak said quickly, seeing her expression. Newly agitated, he got to his feet and began to pace. "See here, I don't know anything about you. I probably shouldn't trust you at all. Usually, I'm damn protective when it comes to Seth. He's been the best friend I've ever had."

"I won't blow his cover."

Kozak stopped pacing and looked at her hard. "You better not."

"He told me there are people looking for him—that he's protecting some secret that could put people's lives in danger. And I know he's a doctor—but not what kind of doctor. Do you know?"

Unwilling, Kozak said, "He was in research."

"What kind of research?"

"I can't tell you more," Kozak said. "The rest of the story has to come from Seth—if he feels like talking."

Pained, Catty shook her head. "I don't think he'll ever confide in me. I haven't given either of you much reason to trust me."

Kozak eyed her for a long moment. "You were ready to protect him from me just now. And by the look in your eye, I have a feeling you wouldn't let anything hurt him."

She snorted. "You going soft on me, Kozak?"

"Hell, no."

"Good. I hate to think too many people were starting to like me. Man, what a day! I could use a drink. How about you?" Catty mustered a grin. "Can I pour you a stiff—oh, Lord. I'm sorry. I forgot."

Kozak shrugged. "Don't worry about it. How about some more coffee?"

"Sure thing." Catty picked up his empty mug. "Say, Kozak?"

"Yeah?"

"You're all right."

"Well," he said, "don't expect me to return the compliment. Not yet, anyway."

When Catty held the door open for Kozak to follow her into the cabin, she caught a glimpse of his face. And she discovered, in that moment, that Mike Kozak had a very nice smile.

Seven

Seth woke up with a headache and a throb in his shoulder and arm that could have lit up a pain meter like a Christmas tree. He swallowed some pain relievers and plopped himself on one of the chairs at the table.

He was glad to see Kozak had arrived, but noticed that the atmosphere between his friend and Catty was a little tense. Still, they seemed capable of civil conversation, and Catty naturally coaxed some laughter out of Mike while they cooked dinner together and served the meal.

Seth sat with them and found he couldn't eat. It wasn't that he wasn't hungry. It wasn't that his shoulder was throbbing or his head ached with a steady thud. He just couldn't take his eyes off Catty. She looked so lovely—blond and fresh and young—as she chatted with Kozak, taunting him and coaxing conversation from him by turns. She smiled and the room seemed to brighten. She laughed, and music wouldn't have sounded more beautiful.

And all her smiles were for Kozak. She couldn't be nicer to the man. She served his dinner and kept his coffee cup full and listened to him talk as if he were explaining the mysteries of the universe. Seth burned inside. He was disgusted. He was angry.

Who was he kidding? He was jealous!

That thought knifed through the fog of muddled-up emotions and struck Seth with such absolute clarity that he actually jumped. He dropped his fork, and it clattered on the table.

In an instant, Catty was on her feet and scurrying around to his side.

"Are you all right?" she asked, bending close over his shoulder with great concern. She laid one arm across his back and touched his forearm with her other hand. "Seth? Are you feeling worse?"

"No." He shook his head. "Ah—I mean, not exactly. I just—for a moment there I felt—"

"We've tired you out," Catty said at once. "We were being thoughtless. Come, let me help you over to the fire, all right? I'll tuck you into some blankets and bring you a glass of wine. How does that sound?"

"Okay," Seth said, allowing her to help him to his feet. He even faked a stumble so she'd hug him harder.

Things would have gone his way perfectly if he hadn't happened to catch the expression on Kozak's face.

"What's the matter with you?" Seth demanded.

"Me?" Kozak endeavored to look innocent. "Why, nothing. I'm not the one who needs a nurse."

"I don't either," Seth growled.

Kozak laughed. "No, I don't think you do, my friend."

"Don't tease him," Catty commanded. "Mike, you're not being nice. Now help me get him over to the couch, will you?"

"He doesn't need to sit down, Catty," Kozak said. "Maybe he just needs some fresh air. Some *cool* fresh air. Take him outside. I'll do the dishes."

"Well..." Catty began doubtfully.

"That's a good idea," Seth said. "We'll just step outside for a few minutes."

"Take your time," Kozak said blandly. But when Catty's back was turned, Kozak waggled his eyebrows at Seth.

With a quelling look thrown over his shoulder, Seth let Catty draw him by the hand into the night air. The porch was wreathed in shadows, and the fresh breeze off the lake sharpened Seth's senses to an acute state of awareness. Catty twirled around before him, her hair floating about her shoulders. Seth caught the scent of her, and it was almost dizzying. She pulled him to the porch railing and perched there, looking up into his face with a sweet frown of concern on her brow.

"Feeling all right?" she asked anxiously.

"Not too bad."

"Tell me the instant you get tired," she ordered. "We'll go back inside."

"I'm not tired. Let's go for a walk."

"Are you kidding?" Her lovely brown eyes widened. "Seth, it's—"

"Come on," he said, gripping her wrist. He could hear Kozak crashing and splashing in the kitchen, and he figured his friend intended to eavesdrop unashamedly. He pulled Catty off the porch, and together they strolled down the path under the fragrant pines.

Beside him, Catty stayed silent. But Seth could sense that she was ready to pop. He had never known Catty to shut up for longer than one minute unless she had something on her mind.

At last, she stepped in front of him and turned. "Seth," she said, abrupt and abrasive, "I'd like to help you. I *can* help you beat whatever you're fighting. Kozak wants it, too. Together, we could do it. I know we can."

Her upturned face looked very young in the moonlight. Her eyes were luminous, yet electric. Seth was moved to touch her cheek, to feel its smooth contour under his fingertips. "There is no 'we' in this situation, Catty," he said. "This is my problem, not yours. I've made that clear, haven't I?"

She grasped his hand and squeezed. "One thing about me—I don't always listen to what I'm told."

He grinned. "I've noticed that."

She didn't smile back. "You can't stay here forever, Seth. Surely you see that. Eventually something's got to give."

"I never intended to hide here forever." Seth put his back against the trunk of a pine, and he leaned there, looking out over the placid lake. The evening seemed to require honesty. He said, "I planned to hole up here for a while and figure out a way to end it all. It was easy, though, staying here. Nobody gets hurt if I keep to myself. My actions affect only me. Do you understand what I'm talking about?"

"Of course. But can't you see what you're doing to yourself?"

"It's not so bad."

"Compared to what? Slow poison?"

Seth smiled again, looking at the determined thrust of Catty's pointed chin. "You know what I mean."

"No, I don't." She pushed away and stood on the path, her fists cocked on her narrow hips. "Okay, you're going to save the world!" she said. "But at what cost? You have so much to give, but you're practically buried here, Seth. You have to get off this island before you molder!"

He laughed shortly. "That's what I like about you, Catty. You never look at the dark side, do you?"

"I always look for a way out, if that's what you mean."

"It is. Somehow, I can't imagine you stuck in any kind of trouble. You're like the fox that's willing to chew its foot off."

"You're right. I hate being trapped. There's always a way out." She trembled, trying hard to suppress her anger. But suddenly she cried, "I hate seeing you here! You're a doctor, for crying out loud! You could be helping starving children someplace or—or taking care of doddering old people! Dammit, what's so important? What makes you think you can't come back to the land of the living?"

"Catty, I—"

"Tell me!"

She had that look on her face again—indefatigable Catty, Catty the fighter, Catty the winner.

"Tell me," she commanded.

It was a secret he'd kept for a long time. There were days when he thought it might eat him up inside, but it hadn't. How many times had he considered telling someone?

Now, here was Catty—a woman who made her career out of meddling. A woman who used information to pull herself up out of poverty. And Seth was tempted to spill everything to her.

He'd felt her touch, seen her naked face, felt the tremors of her body when she surrendered to him. She had trusted him, and now Seth felt as though he could return that trust.

"I don't expect you to understand it all," he started.

"I'm not such an amoral floozy as everybody thinks," Catty countered, raising an eyebrow.

He laughed. "Okay," he said, letting go of his final misgivings. "It's got to do with my father."

"Who's he?"

"Stewart Barnhurst. He's dead."

Catty didn't react—didn't rush to voice empty phrases of condolence. She waited for more, allowing Seth to set his own pace.

Grateful for her silence, Seth touched her hair, a quick caress. He said, "My dad was a research biologist with a company in California. You've probably never heard of it. They do a lot of hush-hush stuff."

"Like what?" Catty shifted closer, listening attentively.

"Research and development for drug companies mostly. But many projects for the government, too. That was my father's area of expertise, at least. When I joined the company—"

"You worked there, too?"

Seth hesitated. "Yes. After I finished med school my father asked me to join his team. I was excited at first. I'd heard bits and pieces about his work for years, and it sounded interesting. It wasn't until I was on the inside that I realized what he was doing."

"Which was?"

"There are lots of words for it. But essentially, he was creating chemicals for use in warfare."

"What do you mean? Like Agent Orange?"

"Products like that, yes—though not specifically."

Catty cursed softly. Her gaze never left Seth's face. "That kind of work doesn't sound like your style."

"You're right," Seth said, and he felt a swell of tenderness for her. Catty was unconditionally loyal. He decided he could tell her the rest and he did in a rush, as if ridding himself of a guilty secret. "I felt—well, I had mixed feelings. After all, this was my father—the one man in the world I admired above all others. I thought we shared the same ideology. Oh, we weren't a very political family. At our house, we discussed medicine at the dinner table, so at first I had no clear opinions about the work I found myself doing. For a while, it was easy to believe the propaganda. My new colleagues—my father and his cronies, the men I used to follow around the golf course, men who brought their families to our house on holidays—suddenly I was hearing them talk about humane methods, about 'quick terminations.' They had euphemisms that made it all sound very clean—like cocktail party conversation. But we were making weapons, Catty. We were looking for quick, inexpensive ways to kill people.''

Seth turned away from her. The past came flooding into his mind, the people and events suddenly clear in his memory. ''We worked in a beautiful big building on the top of a cliff,'' he said, remembering. ''It had been designed by some wonder-boy California architect, and it was lovely. There were beautiful paintings hanging in the corridors, skylights let in the sunshine. The company even paid for a chef to be on the premises seven days a week. We were given every luxury. I guess they thought all the perks would keep us happy.''

''And you'd forget what you were working on.''

''Yes. But I couldn't forget. I—I lasted about a year, and then I started to fall apart, I guess. My father was furious with me after a while. We argued day and night. And my— there was a woman in my life then, too. We'd met in school, and she became a biochemist and worked at the lab, too.''

''Were you lovers?''

For an instant, Seth wished he could deny it. But instead said, ''Yes. We lived together in a community just down the road from the lab. My parents lived on the same street. It was a whole neighborhood of people who worked for the company.''

''Convenient,'' Catty commented. ''For the brainwashing, I mean.''

''You figured that out. Yes, it was brainwashing of a sort. We lived, worked and socialized in a closed society.''

''So when you started to change your mind about your work, everybody in the neighborhood knew it.''

"Exactly. As soon as I made my opinions vocal, I was 'cut out of the loop.' Even our landlady suddenly terminated our lease."

"You were kicked out of the neighborhood of the faithful."

"Right."

"How about the girlfriend?"

"Denise? We split up. She stayed with the company, but after a few months I moved back to Los Angeles. Not long after that, though, my mother called me to come home."

Catty waited for more. When Seth turned his head, his face looked hard in the half light, but his voice told Catty that he wasn't able to relate the rest of the story with complete, cold-blooded calm.

He said, "My father had a heart attack at work, and she was hysterical. I went to help, of course and ended up staying with my family for a few weeks. But Dad didn't last. He hated the thought of prolonging his life with machines, so he came home."

"Oh, Seth."

He shook his head, clearly not wanting to dwell on the emotional aspects of the story. "It happened very quickly. He had another heart attack while watching a football game on television. There was nothing I could do. In those last few minutes together, we made our peace with each other— and he asked me to do something for him."

Half afraid to hear the answer, Catty asked, "What was that?"

"He said that after he was dead, I wasn't to call the ambulance for two hours. And he gave me his passkey to the lab."

"What kind of passkey?"

"For the security system. Every employee was issued one for access to the lab at any time. Dad knew the company would cancel his security code as soon as they knew he was dead, so I had to move fast.''

"You broke in?"

"Yes. It was a Sunday night, and I figured the place would be deserted. I knew the setup, I had his passkey, so it was easy. I opened my father's safe and went through his files. I stole his formulas. He'd been working on some special projects and had even reached the prototype stage.''

"What does that mean?"

"In the safe, I found vials of the product he'd been testing. I stole them along with the formulas. I still have them, in fact.''

Startled, Catty demanded, "Why? For crying out loud, if you'd get rid of the evidence you could never be prosecuted! Seth, you'd be safe if—"

"That's just it, Catty. I can't just dump the vials or bury them. I can't even destroy these chemicals—not without some very sophisticated laboratory equipment. Even a drop of the stuff could pollute this entire lake for decades. My father knew that, but others didn't believe how dangerous it is. He didn't want to risk the chemicals getting loose—or being taken lightly by his colleagues. So I had to take the vials.''

"Where are they?"

"Here. I've packed them as carefully as I know how and hidden them.''

Catty decided she didn't want to know where. "Can anyone prove you were the thief? Did you leave fingerprints? Did someone see you?"

"Yes, to both questions. I did leave fingerprints, though I thought I was being careful. I'd be a terrible spy. And someone did find me in the lab that night, but she didn't turn me in.''

Catty tensed. "She?"

"Yes. It was Denise." Again, Seth looked away. "She was the one who found me."

Catty could scarcely draw a breath. "What did she do?"

"Nothing." Seth shook his head. "That's just it. Denise opened the door and stood there looking at me. Her face showed nothing, but I could guess the turmoil she was feeling at that moment. I was in my father's private office with a flashlight and his open safe. She must have stood in the doorway for two full minutes. She didn't speak, just watched me work. Then she left—just turned around and left me alone to finish the job."

"Did she call the police?"

Seth's mouth was a grim line. "No. And later, when the investigating team questioned her, she never said a word about me. But—she wasn't a convincing liar."

"What do you mean?"

"They knew she wasn't telling the truth. So they concocted a charge against her—something about trading secrets that jeopardized government security."

"That's treason."

"Right. It was supposed to blackmail Denise into revealing me. If I had only known! I heard all this through my mother, months after it all happened." With a quiver of anger in his voice, Seth said, "If I'd known what was going on, I would have turned myself in. I had no idea Denise was trying to protect me."

"What happened to her?"

Seth rubbed his shoulder as if it had started to ache again. His face reflected pain, too, but a different kind. "She went to jail."

"My God."

"Not for treason. They couldn't prove that. It was a lesser charge, but Denise was in a women's correctional facility for nearly a year." Bitterly, Seth said, "It was the same year I had been a fugitive—running all over the country with my gloriously noble cause. I finally settled down here, and my mother was able to make contact with me. She told me what had happened. By that time, Denise had served her time and had been released.''

''Did you try to get in touch with her?''

''Right away. I left the island and made my way to a small town in Wisconsin in case they were tracing all the calls that came into her house. I used a public phone.''

''What did she say?''

''Nothing. Denise hung up on me as soon as she recognized my voice.'' Seth ran his hand through his hair. ''I've tried several times, but her response has always been the same.''

''Her phone is probably tapped.''

''Probably. I wrote to her—Kozak has sent the letters to various members of his family around the country and asked them to mail them so the postmarks wouldn't lead the government agents here. I can't risk giving Denise an address, so she isn't able to write back. I can't imagine what she feels about all of it.''

''She must be trying to get on with her life.''

''I suppose. My mother and I have rigged up a complicated system so we can communicate without getting caught, and she told me last year that Denise was getting married.''

''I see.''

Seth heard her tone of voice and smiled grimly. ''I wasn't heartbroken when I heard that. Our relationship had been over before the whole mess started—we both knew that and had managed to find a comfortable friendship. But I felt— well, I cheated a good friend out of a year of her life. I can't forgive myself for that.''

Catty touched his arm. ''I'm sure she has.''

Seth's jaw was tight. ''I did a terrible thing to her, Catty. It should have been my business, and she shouldn't have been involved. I just—I hope I can apologize to her someday."

"You will. And you'll get out of this mess, Seth. I know you will. I want to help. So does Kozak."

He shook his head. "No."

"Seth, don't be an idiot!" Catty seized his hand. "We can—"

"Dammit, Catty, use your head!" Ferociously, Seth lashed out, "I can't allow anyone else to get mixed up in this. What happened to Denise could take place all over again."

"We'll be careful!"

"You'll have to be. I've told you everything, and that's danger enough. But I won't let you—"

"For heaven's sake, I *can* help! I've got connections! We'll go direct to Washington and—"

"*No,*" Seth snapped. His face looked terrifyingly dangerous for a moment, and he had to choke out the words. "I'm not going anywhere. I never intended to stay here forever, but it's safe for the moment. Don't you see? As long as I stay here, nobody else gets hurt!"

Catty was silent. She allowed Seth time to calm down. Then, softly, she said, "We've got to get rid of the evidence, you know. The vials, I mean. You still have them, you say?"

"Yes." Sounding tired, he said, "But I wasn't kidding before. They're practically impossible to destroy, Catty. I can't just waltz into the nearest high school and light a Bunsen burner to get rid of these compounds. I'm talking about high-tech chemistry, the kind of facilities that only exist in two or three places in the free world. And believe me, those places don't take kindly to tourists, either. Besides, even if I do destroy the prototypes, there's still the matter of the formulas themselves."

"You can burn those!"

"Don't you think I haven't done that already? Trouble is, they're still here." Seth tapped his own head. "I helped create the formulas. I know them."

"Yes, but—! Nobody's going to torture you!" She scoffed at the thought. "Seth, this is America! Nobody is going to stick you with a needle and make you talk." Seeing his expression, she hesitated. "Are they?"

Deadly serious, Seth said, "You don't know what's at stake, Catty. We're talking about chemical compounds that have cost millions to create. And there are people who think they are the answer to world peace—just the way some politicians believe the balance of nuclear weapons will save us all from annihilation."

"That's what you meant when you said the lives of so many people depended on you staying here."

"Yes. Do you understand now? There's nothing I can do."

The wheels began to turn in Catty's mind. She shook her head and declared, "I don't believe in stalemates."

Seth laughed shortly. "I can see that. But this situation is mine, not yours. Until I come up with a perfect plan, I'm staying right here."

Catty turned away, folded her arms and brooded. For her, there was no such thing as a no-win situation.

"You're making me nervous," Seth said at last, sounding amused. "That expression of yours is positively frightening."

She turned when he brushed her shoulder. Then Seth touched her cheek, and Catty glanced up at him, trying to hide her thoughts. If he knew the magnitude of the plan she had already come up with, he'd run screaming for the cabin. So Catty said, "My face always gives me away."

Softly, he replied, "It's a very nice face."

At the change in timbre of his voice, Catty felt herself get warm inside. Her toes and fingertips began to tingle. It wasn't just his voice that affected her. He had finally trusted her. At long last, she didn't feel like his enemy. That realization meant more than any compliment he could ever bestow. Standing there in a shaft of moonlight, looking up at Seth, she wondered if she'd ever felt happier.

Caressing her cheek, Seth leaned closer. "A very, very nice face."

His lips brushed hers. It was hardly a kiss, but it packed a wallop just the same, sending volts of pleasure directly into Catty's brain before easing southward into the warmer regions of her body. Seth brushed his nose against hers, then slowly traced the shape of her cheek, her chin.

Quietly, he said, "You're a tough cookie, Catty Sinclair. I admire your spirit. But this is my affair, not yours. You've got to respect that."

"Y-yes." Catty felt her body grow languorous, as if gently intoxicated by his touch. She closed her eyes and tried to pinpoint exactly how he made her feel. She wanted to memorize the sensation.

He sighed. "I tried not to confide in you, Catty. But there's something about you that makes me—"

"Weak."

He laughed. "I was going to say talkative."

Her eyes flew open. "No, no, I meant that you make *me* feel weak. I can't help it, I just—"

Seth was smiling at her, and his eyes were full of smoke. He said, "I feel weak, too. We should go back inside before we're both overcome by weakness."

"Yes."

A moment ticked by.

"I can't seem to make myself do it." Seth curled one arm around her waist and pulled Catty closer. Appreciatively, he went on skimming her features with his nose, all the while watching her eyes. His own face was suddenly alive with unadulterated desire.

"Wait," Catty whispered, turning her face away from his lips.

"Wait for what?" he murmured, nuzzling her ear.

"I don't know." Catty braced her hands against his good shoulder. Shaky, she said, "I'm just—I was afraid."

"Afraid?"

"That we might do something stupid."

"Like what?"

"Like kiss or something."

"That's stupid?"

"Well, sure," Catty said, though her voice had sunk to an infuriating whisper. "I mean, things are complicated enough already."

"Is one more kiss going to make a difference?"

"It—it might."

With every passing heartbeat, Seth was pulling her closer to him again. "Why?"

"Because one kiss would lead to another," she insisted, "and—and another and then we'd—why, we'd want—"

"To do other things?"

"And say other things. Things we might regret."

"Like what?"

Like I love you. The words were ringing in Catty's head. She knew they were true, but if they burbled out of her mouth, everything would be ruined. She was in love with him. Head over heels. Madly and passionately. But after hearing his story about his former lover and how he regretted hurting her, Catty knew what Seth's reaction would be if she told him what she was feeling. He might throw her off the island without a by-your-leave, and she knew she couldn't bear to be parted from him.

Seth had both arms around her waist, and his right hand was smoothing up her back, as if memorizing every vertebra in her spine. It made her crazy. She wanted more. She wanted to feel his fingertips on her bare skin.

As if reading her thoughts, Seth asked, "What other things would you like to do, Catty?"

"This, for one," she said, sliding her arms around his neck. "And this." She aligned her body to his, relishing the contact with his hard thighs, his taut belly. Her breasts felt electrified by pressing against his chest. It was making her crazy, too. She couldn't think for all the blood that was pounding in her head.

A laugh shook Seth's voice. "What else?"

She began to press kiss after kiss up the length of his throat. "Then I might ask you to reach into my hip pocket."

"Oh, yeah? What's in there?" He needn't have asked, because he was already gently pressing into the pocket to locate the treasure she had secreted there. He brought the small, flat object out into the moonlight, then abruptly loosened his embrace as he held it up for a better look.

"What the hell is this?"

"Can't you tell? I know what it is," Catty said primly, sliding out of his arms completely. "I just can't say the word out loud."

Seth was laughing in earnest by that time, but he caught her hand and pulled her back against his body. "You're a resourceful little witch, aren't you? Where'd you find an open drugstore on a deserted island?"

"I didn't exactly find it," Catty admitted, feeling absurdly shy suddenly. "Can you stand another confession?"

Seth attempted to look stern. "Where did this come from, young lady?"

"I stole it. From Kozak this morning." When Seth began to laugh again, Catty begged, "You won't tell him, will you? Please, Seth, I'm embarrassed enough as it is, but—"

Seth silenced her by taking Catty into the circle of his arm again. He swooped down and pressed a warm kiss to her lips. "I don't kiss and tell, Catty," he said, voice husky. "And for once, I'm glad for your larcenous little heart.

Come with me. I know a perfect spot under the trees where we can make delicious use of this handy little item." He began to pull her into the shadows.

But Catty resisted. "Hold onto your hormones, Doctor."

"Catty! You aren't going to deny a wounded man, are you?"

Catty cocked a severe look up at him. "You bet your bandages. Seth, you've been badly hurt. Heavens, you've lost blood! In your weakened condition, you might—"

"I won't die of making love."

"What if the bear comes back? I might have wounded him and he'll—"

Seth grinned. "We'll scare him off with all the noise we're going to make."

Catty blushed. "Forget it. Besides, I want you in perfect condition when we—when we—"

"Make love."

"Yes, right. Until you can—"

"Say the words for me, Catty."

Startled, she looked up at his face. "What words?"

"Making love. Come on, I want to hear it from your lips. Not any crude euphemisms, either. Tell me what you want to do. Say it for me."

"Okay." She couldn't meet his eye, though. She had to look away. With difficulty, she said, "I'd like—I want to make love with you."

He touched her chin with the point of his finger and tipped Catty's face until her gaze unavoidably met his own. Softly, he said, "Again, please."

Catty could feel her heart hammering in her chest. Inside, other parts of her body began to tremble, too. She was longing for his touch, suddenly aching to feel his hands on her breasts, his clever lips and tongue on her bare skin. His eyes were dark pools of desire, and Catty realize she was melting to dive in. She wet her lips and summoned her voice. "Seth," she whispered, "I do want to make love with you."

He kissed her then, slowly tilting her chin and lowering his own mouth until he hovered just centimeters from her lips. For an achingly long instant, he prolonged the wait, and then he pressed deeply into her mouth with his own. He slipped his hands into her hair and held her head, gyrating his lips until Catty's mouth opened and her tongue melted with sweet sensations. She moaned and felt her heart tear out of control.

Before she knew what she was doing, her own hands were sliding along the muscles of his arms, down the knifelike cut of his waist and hips, gliding to the coarse fabric of his jeans. He felt so wonderful, so hard and so gentle at the same time. She'd never wanted a man like this. Never.

She arched into his body, breathing raggedly, murmuring nonsense, too delirious to make sense of reality. She wanted to drink in the man. Nipping his lips, searching his tongue with her own, she longed to claim him as he had claimed her before. A primitive madness seized her, throbbing in her veins, aching in her heart.

But Seth ended the kiss and gripped her shoulders to hold her back. She turned her eyes up to his. Her voice sounded as strange as the rest of her body felt. She whispered, "I feel so close to you tonight."

"I know. I feel it, too." Seth looked worried. "But—"

"Don't say it," Catty commanded, the wildness dying inside her as quickly as it had arrived.

"How do you know what I was going to say?"

"I know you," she said, drawing out of his arms. "I know your type."

He laughed hoarsely, the urgency of a moment before still discernible in his voice. "What type am I?"

"The noble type. The I'm-no-good-for-you type."

"Catty—"

"I mean it," she snapped fiercely. "I don't want to hear it!" A clog of tears suddenly caught in her throat, and Catty cursed. She couldn't look up at him. If she did, there would be a stupid scene. Catty hated weepy women, and she was damned if she was going to start being one herself. Seth touched her, but she hunched her shoulders and turned away.

Seth said quietly, "It's true, you know."

"Shut up."

Soothing, he said, "My life's a disaster, Catty. The last thing I need right now—"

"I know, I know. Just—just don't expect me to like it!"

"Twenty-four hours ago I'd have said you didn't even like me."

"I don't," she snapped. "I hate your guts. I'm going inside. Kozak will talk to me."

"Catty—"

She shook off his restraining hand. "Don't."

He let her go, then. Catty raced up the path, leaving Seth to fend for himself in the darkness. Choking down sounds that some people might have suspected were sobs, Catty slammed through the door and stormed into the cabin.

Kozak looked up from the book he was reading by the fireside. He took one glance at Catty's face and said mildly, "Lovers' quarrel?"

Catty responded by suggesting an uncomfortable place for Kozak to put his stupid book.

Eight

Seth slept in the bed that night. Kozak and Catty shared the floor by the fire. Catty didn't care how uncomfortable it was this time or that the dogs curled up next to her. She spent the night thinking. Planning. There had to be a way out for Seth.

In the morning, Kozak got up early and made coffee. Catty dragged herself out of her blanket half an hour later. It quickly became apparent to her that Kozak wasn't a morning conversationalist, because he drank his coffee and went outside to look at the sunrise. Catty made breakfast with the adoring dogs underfoot.

Seth woke up an hour or so later and came down the stairs looking alert and so attractively tousled from his bed that Catty found she couldn't speak for a moment. He smiled and advanced upon her as lithely as a cat, taking Catty into his arms and kissing her warmly on the mouth.

"Morning," he murmured against her lips.

She smiled, and he smiled, and they stood for a while in a pool of morning sunshine that slanted through the window. Time seemed to suspend itself while a warm glow radiated through Catty's entire body.

Seth said, "Forgive me for last night?"

"There's nothing to forgive. We were both under the influence of—of something."

"Yes."

"How do you feel?" Catty asked at last.

"Terrible," Seth cheerfully replied, cradling her in his arms. "Like a coyote has been gnawing on my shoulder half the night. But my chest is just itchy and my headache is reduced to a dull thud, so I'm going to live. I just need a day of TLC, and I'll be good as new."

Catty couldn't resist smiling up at him. "You're sure of that diagnosis, Doctor?"

"Positive." Arching his brows hopefully, he said, "All I need is a willing nurse—somebody who could tuck me into bed again with strict orders not to get up until noon."

"Maybe I should apply for the position."

"What kind of experience do you have, Miss?"

"Not much. But I'm willing."

"I could teach you the fine points." He began to trace patterns on her back, delicious caresses.

"I'd like that," Catty said softly, her eyes half closed. She wanted to absorb everything about that moment—the sunlight, her own lazy heartbeat, Seth's strong body, his playful tone of voice.

Pulling her closer, he said, "Maybe we should get started right away. Uh—is Kozak still here?"

Remembering reality, Catty laughed and slipped out of Seth's embrace. "Yes, indeed. I think he's afraid to leave you alone with me. He's on the porch, no doubt eavesdropping in case I try to hurt you again."

Seth sighed.

On cue, Kozak pulled open the screen door and came inside. He didn't bother with good-mornings, but said in a low, tense voice, "Someone's coming."

"Who?"

"Small boat. Two people. They're coming around the point right now."

Already on her way out the door, Catty said to Seth, "Stay here. Keep out of sight."

He was going to disobey, but as he started to follow Catty, Kozak barred Seth's way. "She's right," Kozak said. "If it's trouble, I'll pretend I'm you. Got it?"

Catty leaned out over the balcony to get a glimpse of the newcomers. The dogs followed her, Sam putting his paws up on the railing as if to take a look, too. Catty put one hand up to shield her eyes from the blaze of sunshine and the dazzle of the water. In a moment, she made out the oncoming boat and quickly saw that it was her friend, the freckle-faced kid from Bob's Bait and Tackle, the boy who'd taken her message yesterday.

Sitting in the bow of his boat was another man. At first Catty didn't recognize him, but she hurried down the path and walked out onto the dock with the two dogs at her heels. As the boat drew closer, she felt a stab of horror in her heart.

"My God," she muttered. "It's Royce."

Reggie Royce, top reporter for the same New York newspaper that occasionally sent Catty on the trail of sensational news stories. Royce had a reputation for being tough.

"He's slime," were the actual words people used when they talked about Reggie Royce. "Watch out for him."

What in hell was Royce doing here?

Suddenly Catty knew. And it terrified her.

She saw a paddle stowed on Kozak's boat, and by instinct, she reached for it. Then she stood on the dock with her heart pounding as the boat drew closer, holding the paddle as if it could protect them all from what was coming.

The kid waved. "Hi, Miss Sinclair! I did what you asked me to do!"

"Thanks a heap," Catty muttered before the boat came within earshot.

Reggie Royce sat in the bow of the rocky little boat, clutching the gunwales for support. He made no attempt to help dock the craft, but when the kid steered the boat against the dock, he jumped out quickly.

He had a smile like a crocodile—lots of tiny little teeth in a very wide mouth that was open in an oily kind of grin. He was dressed inappropriately in loose trousers and a tweed jacket with an unraveled spot on one sleeve. His sunglasses were tinted pink.

"Hi," he said, sounding jaunty. "Catty Sinclair, right? We met a couple of years ago at Margo Swensen's party. I'm Reggie Royce."

"Yeah, sure." Catty ignored the handshake he extended. "What are you doing here?"

It seemed that Royce was as ready as she was to drop the pleasantries. He pulled a pack of cigarettes from his jacket pocket and got down to business. "I talked with your assistant yesterday."

"Sharon? What did she tell you?"

Royce grinned and tapped a cigarette out of the pack. "About the Barnhurst story."

"The what?"

He laughed. "Sure, sure. Your assistant was doing research for you, right? Well, she needed some help yesterday, and pretty soon the word got around."

"What are you talking about?"

"Your assistant. She spilled the beans."

Catty nearly screamed. How stupid could she have been? Sharon had unwittingly let something slip and now Seth's name was being blasted all over the research department of one of New York's leading newspapers! Seth's whereabouts were probably known halfway around the world!

Desperate, Catty began to bluff. "I don't know what you're talking about, Royce. Sharon must have gotten the name wrong. I was sent here to look for a rock-and-roll singer—Rafer Fernando."

"Don't give me that, Sinclair."

"Give you what? What's this other guy you're talking about? Barnstable?"

"Don't bother pulling that act on me. The name is Barnhurst, as you very well know." Royce lit up his cigarette, blew smoke and began to look less pleasant. "Don't get your dander up. The editor said you're not the best writer for this story. So I'm here to interview Barnhurst and get his side. I'll split the byline with you if you're going to get touchy. Where is he?"

Catty backed up a pace. "I don't know what you're talking about."

"You don't?" Royce leaned closer and deliberately blew smoke in Catty's face. "Listen, honey, you're sitting on a hot piece here. You want it for yourself? Fine. I can dig it. But you're going to have to share access to Barnhurst eventually. I mean, he's going to be very hot news soon, and you can't keep him under wraps forever. This place is going to be swarming with reporters by nightfall. Now, I've got to file by six o'clock, so let's—"

"Get out," Catty said. She brandished the paddle.

Royce looked startled, but not undaunted. "Oh come on, honey—"

"I mean it." With her hand, Catty shoved Royce in the chest, and he staggered backwards.

"Hey!"

"Clear out!" Catty shouted. "This is private property. Get off this island before I set the dogs on you!"

For good measure, Sam began to growl.

Royce, looking stunned, stared at the dog, then at Catty. "Are you serious? You really think you can keep Barnhurst to yourself?"

"Get out of here!" Catty screamed. With the paddle, she took a swat at him for good measure. "Go on!"

Royce threw his cigarette into the lake and scuttled for the boat. He climbed in, but sent Catty a murderous look.

"I'll be back," he said. "I'll fix it so you're swamped with press. You can't get away with this, Sinclair."

The kid in the boat looked stunned, but scared. When Catty threw him some bills to cover the cost of the errand she'd sent him on, he was too amazed to thank her. He jammed the engine into reverse and cleared out fast.

Catty ran up the path and charged into the cabin. Inside, she rocked to a stop, panting hard. "We've got to get out of here."

Brusquely, Kozak said, "We heard everything."

They were already packing, hastily assembling enough gear to make an escape. Without a word, Seth was stuffing an extra sweater into a nylon duffel bag. Beside him, Kozak was checking a box of shells and setting out the guns. Neither man looked at her.

"I'm sorry," Catty said, suddenly very frightened.

Seth said, "It's done now."

Catty hurried to him, then didn't have the courage to touch him. "Seth, you've got to believe. I didn't know this was going to happen."

"It did," Kozak snapped.

Catty grabbed the edge of the table to keep from flinging herself into Seth's arms and begging for forgiveness. Trying to keep the crack out of her voice, she said, "It was an accident. I sent a letter to my assistant in New York yesterday. I told her it was secret, I just wanted some information, that's all. It was instinct!"

"Yeah," Kozak said grimly. "Now the wolves are howling, aren't they? Nice job, Miss Sinclair."

Seth never looked at Catty. He turned to Kozak. "I have to go through the house. There are bound to be papers, letters—I don't know what else. I can't leave that kind of evidence—"

"I'll do it," Kozak said. "You have to get out of here fast. What about the stuff?"

"I'll take the vials with me. I'll head for the campsite we used last spring, remember? On the north side of Gull Island."

"Yeah. I'll bring the plane tonight after I've cleaned up here. If we're lucky, we'll be a hundred miles away by morning."

They were acting like she wasn't even in the room.

"Bring the dogs," Seth said. "I can't leave them here."

"I will."

"And the books, you'll have to go through the books. Hell, it will take all day, but I may have left notes between the pages. Mike, maybe we'd better just torch the place."

"Set fire to it? Seth, this has been in your family for generations. You can't—"

Catty said, "The two of you are acting really stupid."

They looked at her.

"I mean it," she said. "If a mob of reporters shows up here and finds a burned-up cabin, what are they going to think? That you're guilty, of course. You don't know what kind of lengths they'll go to to find you. They'll hire helicopters. They'll—"

Kozak snapped, "I'll have him out of here before they can mobilize—"

"Oh, stop talking like a weekend warrior! It's too late for that. The story's already in progress. If you disappear, you'll just make the story bigger."

Seth said, "What do you suggest?"

Kozak swung around and sputtered, "Don't ask her! She's the enemy! She's one of them!"

"Exactly," Catty said calmly. "So I know how they'll think. I can help."

"How?" asked Seth.

"There's only one way to kill a story of this magnitude," Catty told them. "And that's to create an even bigger story."

"Like what?" Kozak demanded coldly. "You planning to declare war on the north pole or something?"

"No, I've got something bigger than that."

Seth was watching her face. "Rafer Fernando."

"Who?" Kozak asked. "Wait, you mean the dead guy?"

"Show me how to use the phone," Catty said to Seth.

He said, "Do you really expect your idea to work?"

"Sure. I'll make a couple of calls, tell people that I've spotted Rafer Fernando—here and alive. I guarantee it, there will be hysterical fans flocking all over this lake before noon."

"That'll just make things worse!" Kozak cried. "It'll be—"

"It'll be safe," Catty interrupted. "We can hide in a crowd. The more people, the easier it will be to slip away. And judging by the number of people who still believe that Fernando is alive, I think we'll be hip deep in rock-and-roll fans in no time."

Musingly, Seth said, "It sounds crazy enough to work."

"Are you nuts?" Kozak grabbed Seth's shirt. "How can you stand there and listen to her with a straight face? She's the cause of all your troubles!"

"She's not the cause," Seth said, gently disengaging Kozak's grip. "I did that to myself. Catty's made one mistake, that's all. Let's give her a chance to fix things."

Catty felt her eyes start to sting as she looked gratefully at Seth.

Kozak blew a disgusted sigh. "Now I've heard everything."

"Not quite everything," Catty said, pulling herself together. "Here's the deal. Mike, you stay here and clean out anything that could possibly prove that Seth is the man the press is looking for. Burn it. Or wrap everything up in a plastic bag and sink it into the lake for safekeeping. Then sit out on the porch for the rest of the day and pretend you're Seth Bernstein."

"Are you kidding?"

"I mean it. How many people up here can actually identify Seth? Just act like yourself, deny everything—but most important, *stall the press*."

Seth said, "I'll make a camp on Gull Island and wait for Kozak to show up tonight. If anyone stops to question me in the meantime, I just claim I'm a Fernando fan, right?"

"Right. Seth, have you got a portable radio?"

"A—? Sure."

"Good. Every radio station in the country will soon be playing nothing but Rafer Fernando songs. You've got to look like an authentic fan. Too bad we don't have an old Fernando T-shirt or something. Oh, well. Now—somebody tell me how to dial this telephone."

With Kozak's less than willing assistance, Catty began placing phone calls. She started with the big newspapers—in New York, Chicago, Los Angeles and Houston. Then she called a couple of close friends—one in television, the other in radio—and asked them to start spreading the Fernando story. Her most important contact was with a Florida-based tabloid.

"I'm killing my reputation," she muttered between calls. Kozak was nearby. "What?"

She shook her head. "Nothing. It was time for a career change, anyway. Hello, Marsha? Yeah, this is Cathy Sinclair. Fasten your seatbelt, sweetie, have I got some news for you!''

In half an hour, the ball was rolling. The final touches were calls to a couple of local taverns, a restaurant in Deer Lick, and a college radio station less than fifty miles away.

"If that doesn't get the traffic going on this lake, nothing will,'' Catty told Seth and Kozak.

"Let's get a head start,'' Seth suggested. "We'd better leave immediately.''

"We?'' Catty repeated, suddenly shaken by what she thought she'd heard. "You mean, you want me to—?''

"What's my other option? If I leave you here—''

"I won't tell anyone where you've gone. I wouldn't do that.''

"Just the same,'' said Seth. "I want you with me.''

"You still don't trust me, do you?''

Seth said, "I've got a limited number of choices, Catty.''

Kozak said to her, "Quit while you're ahead, kid.''

"I want to hear it.'' Catty steeled herself for a great pain, lifting her chin and marshaling her expression. "Do you trust me or not, Seth?''

"I don't,'' Seth said frankly. "How can I? You're a loose cannon, Catty. I can't guess what you'll do next.'' He hesitated. "But I do believe your heart's in the right place.''

A wretched pain pierced Catty's heart, but she gathered her self-control and said, "I've made some stupid mistakes. And I might again—''

"You might,'' Seth agreed coldly. He touched her cheek, scanning her face with a frightening intensity in his black eyes. "But I'm counting on you otherwise.''

She swallowed the lump in her throat. "I won't let you down, Seth.''

He nodded. "Come on, then. Grab your stuff. We'll take my boat.''

Nine

Francie O'Toole was a waitress at the Dew Drop Inn just twenty-two miles outside of Minneapolis. In her years slinging plates and pouring coffee, she had never seen a crowd the likes of which started pouring into the restaurant on Friday morning.

"Holy cow," she panted as she rested against the milk-shake machine. "What's going on, Morris? Are the volunteer firemen putting on another parade or something?"

Morris, the short-order cook, always worked with a cigar between his teeth, which rendered him incapable of speech. To answer Francie's question, he shook his head and pointed his greasy spatula toward the radio.

But all Francie could hear was an old Rafer Fernando song playing on the radio. She threw an exasperated look at the back of Morris's head, then grabbed a couple of fishburger specials off the hot-counter and carried them down to a table by the window. She was just reaching to set one of the specials down in front of a customer when she heard a snippet of conversation at the next table.

"I can't believe it, can't believe it, can't believe it," gushed an attractive blond girl in a sloppy college sweatshirt. Francie always noticed things like that—a girl with a pretty face ought to have enough sense not to dress like some kind of football player. The girl was leaning across the table to her companion, a long-haired boy who looked equally unkempt. "I just *can't* believe it," she said again. "He's really alive! Justin, why don't we go look for him? You and me! Why, it's the best chance we'll ever get to meet Rafer Fernando!"

Francie dropped the second fishburger special on the floor. The plate crashed on the linoleum of the Dew Drop Inn, French fries skittered in all directions, and the fish sandwich landed mayo-side down on Francie's foot.

But she didn't notice.

"Rafer Fernando!" she screamed. "He's alive?"

At a gas station forty miles north of Kalamazoo, Michigan, a mechanic by the name of Gordie Walters wiped his hands on a garage rag and decided to quit his job.

"I'm sorry, Clarence," he said to his boss. "I gotta go see if I can find that Rafer Fernando guy."

Clarence, his boss, was not pleased. "Goshdarnit, Gordie, we've got six sets of winter tires to change before lunch, and I'm short-handed already!"

"I'm sorry," Gordie said stubbornly. "But I gotta go."

"Gordie, don't you know a hoax when you hear one? How can that Fernando fella be alive? I mean, I thought they buried him!"

Gordie just shook his head. "I don't know about that, Clarence. All I know is my wife is Fernando's biggest fan. She's even got his poster hung up over the bathtub so she can soak in there and look up at that guy."

"But, Gordie," said his boss, looking pained and uncomfortable. "Your wife ran off with Buddy Dunwiley. She's hardly even yours to worry about anymore."

"I know that. But I love her. And if I can talk to Rafer Fernando, she'll take me back," Gordie said. "I just know she will! My mind's made up, Clarence. I'm gonna go right now. It's my only chance to save my marriage. See you around."

Clarence sighed mournfully and thought about six sets of steel-belted radial tires that needed attention and the six irate customers who were going to raise holy hell. The one thing in the world Clarence hated most was irate customers. He always broke out in hives when customers started yelling at him.

"Hey, Gordie!" Clarence shouted. "Wait for me!"

In the town of Deer Lick, chaos reigned. The townspeople never imagined their small community might become the focal point of one of the biggest manhunts in the United States of America. Main Street was clogged with cars. Frantic Fernando fans thronged the beach, launched boats, played their radios and set off across the lake toward the chain of small islands where they believed their hero was hiding.

The Nedwick twins set up a lemonade stand and sold out in forty-five minutes. Mrs. Pasternak, a grouchy old widow who hadn't left her house in four years, except for the time the ambulance took her to the hospital to get the carrot-peeler out of her hand, doddered out onto her porch and was immediately offered twenty dollars for the old, rotting canoe that had been leaning against her garage for at least a decade. Mrs. Pasternak might have been old, but she wasn't stupid. She took a look at the traffic roaring past her house and bargained them up to forty-two dollars before she let the canoe go.

And the three MacLean brothers, who owned a marina as well as Bob's Bait and Tackle, also knew a gold mine when they saw one. They began to rent out boats at triple the normal rate. They sat on their camp chairs outside the boathouse that served as the bait-and-tackle shop and drank soda pop while watching the show. Pretty soon three identical station wagons with government plates pulled up—each towing an aluminum fishing boat with a powerful engine.

"What d'you bet?" said Bob MacLean, watching while six tall, handsome young men got out of the cars and set about launching their fine boats into the water. "Ten bucks says those guys are the FBI."

"What would the FBI want with a rock-and-roll singer?" demanded his brother Jesse.

"Drugs, maybe," Bob suggested. "All those famous people are into drugs."

"Not all of 'em," Jesse said, who was currently suffering a terrible crush on Loni Anderson.

Joey MacLean, the youngest brother, wandered away to check out the action on Main Street. He was soon accosted by three wild-eyed young women who offered a hundred dollars for him to guide them to Rafer Fernando.

"Wait 'til somebody offers you five hundred," his brother Bob advised when Joey came back to announce the deal.

And somebody did. He was a burly man in a khaki outfit that had more pockets and epaulets than a dog has fleas. He wore an Australian bushman's hat with a bristle of stiff little feathers sticking out of the brim, and a leather holster with a real gun snapped into it. The MacLean brothers stood there blinking at the man like he had landed from Mars.

"My name's Pompowsky," the man said importantly. "I've got urgent government business to attend to, and I need a native guide immediately."

"Well, Joey's no injun," drawled Jesse MacLean, "but he knows his way around the lake. What's so urgent, bub?"

"It's Colonel to you," Pompowsky snapped. "And you can mind your own beeswax, young man. Have we got a deal? Let's get the show on the road. Where's the boat?"

Joey was a little dubious about his passenger, who insisted on standing in the bow of the boat like he was Washington crossing the Delaware. But a near capsize finally convinced Pompowsky to sit properly.

"I'm looking for a man by the name of Barnhurst," Pompowsky said to Joey as they pulled toward the deep channel of the lake. "You know him?"

"N-no, sir."

"He might be going by Bernstein these days."

"Oh!" Joey said. "Mr. Bernstein. I know where he is. Boy, he's sure been busy lately!"

"Oh?"

"Yeah, I just took a lady over there the other day."

"I see," said Pompowsky. "Well, you can tell me about her while we make the trip."

"I thought maybe you were looking for Rafer Fernando, sir."

"The United States Army has no interest in that matter."

"Well, it's the biggest thing to ever hit this town," Joey said eagerly. "Why, my brothers and me have made over four hundred dollars already today."

"Make your money today, boy. Tomorrow the whole thing will blow over."

Joey was startled. "Why?"

"It's a diversion, pure and simple. The army knows a diversion when it sees one. Does this rust bucket go any faster, kid? I intend to close this matter before nightfall."

Seth and Catty met their first Fernando fans at two o'clock in the afternoon as their boat rounded the point of a small island and they nearly cut a wobbly canoe into two pieces. Only Seth's quick reactions saved the people from a dunking.

"Hey," shouted the young man who was struggling ineptly with a paddle. He had two cameras slung around his neck and they crashed against the paddle with every stroke he took. "Have you spotted Rafer yet?"

"Not yet," Catty bellowed back through cupped hands. "How about you?"

"Not yet! But I've got a job with a magazine for pictures, so if you see Rafer, tell him that I can negotiate a good deal for him. My name's Morton McCloskey."

"If we see him, we'll tell him," Catty promised.

Seth steered his boat around the canoe, and when they were safely out of range, he said to Catty, "It's working!"

"Of course it's working." She flashed him a confident grin. "I know what I'm doing, you know."

But later in the day, she wasn't so sure. She had noticed that the traffic on the lake had picked up dramatically and there were as many as three helicopters in sight at any given moment. The buzz of boat engines drowned the peaceful silence of the area. But it was the deep, rumbling engine of one particular boat that sounded most businesslike. At the sight of them, she reached for Seth's knapsack—in which he had hidden the vials of toxic chemicals—and tucked it under a rolled-up sleeping bag.

Two men in a low aluminum boat flagged down Seth. He obediently cut his engine, and the two crafts bobbed within a few yards of each other.

"Afternoon, folks," said the man in the bow. "Can I ask you for some ID?"

"Why?" Catty asked. "Are you the police or something?"

The man obligingly flashed a shield. "FBI," he said.

"Wow! What have we done wrong, officer?"

"Nothing, miss. We're just keeping an eye on the area today to make sure nobody gets hurt. You two fishing today?"

"Oh, no," Catty gushed. "We're looking for Rafer Fernando! Do you know where he's staying? We'd love to meet him! We're his biggest fans, aren't we, honey?"

"Hmm," said Seth.

Catty gulped. She hadn't expected that Seth might be a poor actor and realized she was on her own. She turned to them excitedly. "And I'm just dying to get Rafer's autograph! Why, he's just about the best singer in the whole world after Mick Jagger, don't you think?"

"Absolutely," said the FBI man. "Now about that ID?"

"Gee, I'm really sorry," Catty babbled. "But we did a dumb thing this morning. We're just a couple of city kids and we—well, we—"

"Capsized the boat," Seth chimed in. "Turned it right over."

"Yes, we lost just about everything," Catty added. "Our wallets, our credit cards—all that important stuff! Why, all we've got left is this picnic basket and—why, would you two nice gentlemen like a taste of my nasturtium muffins? They're my specialty, and I just know Rafer Fernando will love them—he's a vegetarian, you know, and I just crumbled up some nasturtiums into a mixture of—"

"You both lost your wallets?"

"That's right."

"How come you're not wet?"

"Why, why—"

"We've been sitting in the sun all day," Seth said. "I'm still a little damp underneath."

"Me, too," Catty said eagerly. "Why, if you don't believe me, you can just feel my panties." She hauled her shirttail out from the waistband of her trousers. "Here, you can see right here that I'm still—"

"Darlin'," Seth said, "keep your clothes on. When are you going to get it through your head that everybody isn't dying to see you in your birthday suit?"

Catty sputtered convincingly. "I never thought any such thing! Why, you're mean to say that to me! I have a mind to leave you flat! These nice gentlemen would be delighted to take me home, I'm sure. Wouldn't you, mister? I won't be a speck of trouble. Can I come with you?"

"Uh, we've got official business to take care of," said the FBI man, looking appalled by the suggestion. "You folks just have a pleasant day, all right?"

When the boat was out of sight, Catty realized she was as tense as a watchspring. Then she felt Seth's hand on hers, and she turned to see a look of admiration on his face.

He said, "You can be a pain in the neck when you put your mind to it. Those guys couldn't get out of here fast enough!"

"It worked, didn't it?"

Maybe Seth couldn't help himself. He smiled. "Yes, it did. You're a remarkable lady, Catty Sinclair."

He pulled her against him, then, and Catty sat with her back braced against his chest. Seth steered the boat out onto open water, and the fresh breeze blew in their faces. But it wasn't the air that caused Catty to feel renewed. She nestled against Seth's frame and wondered if they could just stay in the boat forever.

They arrived at the campsite in the late afternoon. The island was even smaller than the one that had been Seth's home for the past several years, but it looked pretty. Seth knew where to beach the boat, and Catty helped him conceal it under some low-hanging boughs of a hemlock tree.

"We'll stay under the trees in that grove up there," he told Catty, pointing to a grassy knoll covered with tall pines. "It's sheltered, and we'll be invisible from the air. Let's set up a camp. We'll have some shelter that way, in case Kozak can't get here by nightfall.''

"What can I do?"

"Let's haul this gear up to the trees." Seth slung his knapsack with its precious cargo over his shoulder. Catty could see that his arm was giving him some pain, so she eagerly pitched in to help.

She dragged the equipment they needed from the boat to the spot Seth had selected and helped organize things. But Catty soon proved to be all thumbs with the tent. Seth took over without remarking upon her inadequacies.

Eventually, Catty gave up trying to help and walked down to the lake. She looked out at the water as the fading sunlight turned it to the color of molten lead. Or maybe it was her heart that felt as though it had been melted in the past couple of days. She shook her head ruefully, then cast a glance over her shoulder. For a few minutes, she watched Seth set up the camp to his liking. His shoulder was stiff, she could see, but he worked easily, his body graceful and efficient. Just watching him, Catty felt a queer thud inside herself. She turned away and frowned at the lake, trying to sort out her feelings. Now that she was alone with him, she began to realize it was probably the last she'd ever see of Seth Barnhurst. Inside, she ached with the thought.

In time, Seth brought her some coffee poured into the lid of the thermos.

"Thanks," she said, accepting his offering and trying to put on a brave front.

"It's the last hot drink you'll have today," Seth said. "So enjoy. We can't risk building a fire tonight."

"Will Kozak be able to find us in the dark?"

"Sure, he knows the area. But he may wait until morning now. If he goes out after dark, his running lights will draw attention."

"He'll leave me here, won't he?"

Seth looked at her and must have seen that Catty wanted the unvarnished truth. "Probably," he said. "Kozak will take me somewhere and come back for you later. He won't want you following me."

"What about you?"

Seth sighed. "Catty—"

"All right, all right. I know you want to disappear with your glow-in-the-dark test tubes." She lifted her chin, hoping he hadn't guessed how emotional she was feeling. Wryly, she said, "This is the last I'll see of you, isn't it?"

Seth touched her face—a quick brush, that's all it was, but Catty felt herself react with a quake that rocked her to her toes. Inside, he must have struggled to find the right words. But he looked tired, Catty could see. The lines in his face looked deeply etched, and by the knot in his brow, she could see that his wounds from yesterday were aching. The last thing he needed now was pressure from an emotional female.

Contrite at once, Catty pressed the cup of coffee into his hands.

"Here. Have some," she said brusquely. "You didn't take any for yourself, did you?"

He shook his head. "I'm all right."

"I insist. Don't cross me, pal. I can be mighty unpleasant when I don't get my way. In case you haven't noticed."

Seth smiled a little and accepted the coffee. "You're a terror, Catty. I admire you for it."

Catty glanced away. Was it possible? A couple of days ago, that kind of praise would have set her aglow.

He drank some of the hot coffee, watching her. Then, softly, Seth said, "What are you thinking?"

She shook her head, too wrought up to speak.

He turned her by her arm until she faced him. "Tell me."

"It's nothing." She kept her head down.

Seth forced her to look at him. "Spill it," he commanded, and his expression compelled her to obey.

Catty took a deep breath to steady herself. "I—I just—I think you should know that I'm not as—as tough as you think I am."

Seth didn't laugh. Quietly, he said, "I know you're not tough, Catty."

"I wish I could be! I wish I wasn't such a marshmallow inside, but I am. And with you, the—the marshmallow part is closer to the surface."

"I'm glad. It's the part I like best about you."

"Don't," Catty burst out, turning away. "Don't talk like that, will you? No mushy stuff."

"All right then, no mushy stuff," he said behind her. "Just the truth. I like you, Catty. You're an exciting woman. Under different circumstances, things might have been different for us."

"Please—"

He moved closer, grasping her shoulders in his hands. "I want more time with you. I want to learn everything about you. I want to talk with you, cook with you, sleep with you—I want it all."

"But we haven't got the time. It's over before it got started."

"Not completely over," Seth said. "We've got tonight."

Catty trembled. His low murmur touched a secret place inside herself, his body radiated wonderful heat, his hands communicated a delicious strength she couldn't resist.

"It's my fault things have worked out so badly," Seth said softly. "I take full responsibility. I could have chased you off the island that first day, but I didn't. I could have taken you to Deer Lick myself, but I didn't do that either. I could have done lots of things to kill what was happening between us, Catty, but I couldn't. I should apologize, but I won't. Tonight I'm more sorry that I didn't act on what I was really feeling for you."

Frighteningly breathless, Catty said, "What are you really feeling?"

Seth bent close so that his lips brushed her ear, his nose ruffled her hair. "Like making love with you," he murmured. "Like taking advantage of this last chance together. I've wanted you, Catty. I've wanted you so badly that it hurts."

Catty turned in his arms. "Why are we wasting time with all this talk, then? Talking hasn't gotten us anywhere so far, has it?"

"Catty—"

"No, none of that noble stuff please. I want it, too. I want to make love in a hundred different ways so you'll remember me for the rest of your life."

"And you," said Seth, "are going to remember me, my love. This is one night you'll never forget."

Ten

Seth's head was filled with fuzzy fantasy—he was too tired to think things through. His body was wide awake, though, and he pulled Catty hard against him to quench a need that roared suddenly out of his subconscious and into his veins. He pressed against her, making no secret of his aroused state—of how badly he wanted her. Catty gasped as she made contact with him.

But she met his kiss halfway, her lips warm and sweet and trembling just a little. With a rhythmic nudge, Seth parted her mouth in one long, searching kiss. He thrust his tongue into the depths of her mouth, running his hands up into the tangle of her long hair and holding her head inescapably. She held him, too, weaving her fingers into his hair and pouring her soul into the kiss. Her small body arched into his, her soft curves fitting exquisitely into his chest, his belly, his thighs. Seth groaned deep in his throat as a keen rush of desire welled inside him.

He needed her—all of her—and quickly. Sweet, vulnerable Catty. She tried so hard to be bad, but inside she was so good. She wanted to be tough, but she followed her heart unerringly. Seth wanted to share in her sweetness, he wanted to find her core, the center of the woman he'd come to know.

Seth released her mouth, leaving her gasping. She threw her head back, laughing recklessly, exposing her throat to him. The sound of her happiness acted like a potent aphrodisiac, sending a gush of pure pleasure out of Seth's heart to the roots of everything in him that was male. He kissed her throat, alternately closing his teeth very gently on her skin and pressing his lips against her warm flesh. He was almost incoherent with desire.

"Catty, love, you're making me crazy. Stop before I hurt you."

"You won't hurt me." Her voice quivered with wonder, and her eyes shone with an intoxicating radiance. "Teach me. Everything, please!"

He laughed raggedly. "A hundred different ways?"

"Yes, and more!"

With one hand, he found the hem of her sweater and moved inside, murmuring to her in nonsensical whispers. Her breast was perfectly fitted for his cupped hand, and his fingers found her nipple instinctively. He squeezed and rolled the little bud, then suddenly wanted to taste her. He pulled Catty down to kneel in the grass and quickly worked her sweater up and off. The pale sunlight bathed her bare breasts in a warm glow. Seth pressed his mouth to one, then the other. Catty's soft cries spurred him to suckle her impatiently.

In a matter of heartbeats, Seth knew he was out of his head. He wanted to tear her clothing, to find the warm center of her body. He longed to push her down and take her with all the ferocity of a wild animal. He felt the stiffening breeze off the lake on his hot skin and realized she had stripped him of his shirt. His fingers fumbled at his belt.

"My God," he said, choking on a desperate laugh. "I'm going to take you here in the grass. This is no good. I'll scare the hell out of you."

"Nobody scares the hell out of me," she replied, panting and laughing at the same time.

But she looked nervous—a pink blush burning on her cheeks, her chest quivering as she gasped for breath. Seth snatched her into his arms. She was light as an angel, and he carried her up the hillside to the grove of trees. Catty's hair tangled around his head. Her perfume was intoxicating. The sparkle of her eyes dazzled him, her bare skin teased his chest. The sight of her full, upturned breasts filled him with rampant desire.

"How did I hold out this long?" Seth growled.

"I don't know, I don't know," Catty breathed.

He unfurled the sleeping bag with a snap and opened it wide. Kneeling before her then, Seth began to undress Catty. His hands were shaking, though, and he wanted to cover every inch of her skin with kisses, lavish her body with caresses. Progress was slow, but in time Catty stood in the fading glow of sunlight, her skin looking like pearl, her hair blowing like a cloud around her shoulders, teasing her bare breasts. She looked beautiful standing shyly there, and for a moment, Seth drank in the vision she made. Then he cupped her buttocks and drew circles on her flesh, using his hands and mouth to tease the timid shadow from her eyes. He licked and nipped, calling up every trick to make her join him in the urgent quest for fulfillment. She shivered at first, then small sounds began to escape her throat and she strained against him. Soon she gripped his shoulders with her hands, urging Seth to delve deeper still with his tongue. He used his fingers to part a path inside her, and when he

knew for certain that she was ready, he drew her down on
the sleeping bag.

Watching his face, settling trustingly into his arms, Catty
obeyed his silent commands. She helped him put on the
protection, then lay back and parted her creamy thighs when
he urged them with his knee. She wound her slender arms
around his neck and pulled him down, breathing in excited
bursts.

"Let me touch you," she said, reaching for him.

Seth shuddered with desire as her gentle hand closed
around him. But he shook his head. "No, don't. Any more
of that, and I won't be able to have you fast enough. I don't
want to hurt you, Catty. We'll take it slow. You've got to
want me more than anything, love."

"I'll die without you." Her eyes were dilated and beautifully liquid. Beneath him, her body moved in an urgent
undulation. He could feel her muscles trembling. The sight
of her heightened arousal sent fire bolts of excitement along
his nerve endings.

Unable to restrain himself, Seth moved to enter her. "I
want you, too," he said, holding his breath. "I can't hold
back. Next time, I'll make it good for you, Catty, I promise, but please—"

He thrust inside and felt Catty tighten exquisitely around
him. Her whole body tensed, then arched. Seth froze,
thinking he had hurt her. But when Catty cried out, he knew
it was not pain, but pleasure that tore the sound from her
throat. His entry alone had sent her over the edge. She con-
vulsed around him, her face naked as the quick, unex-
pected release seized her.

In that moment, Seth knew Catty was his forever. Her
expression—wild and abandoned and feminine—would be
indelibly etched in his mind.

He marveled at her, how instinctively she needed, how
freely she gave her body to him. Her passion engulfed him,

her spirit invaded him. She was binding herself to him, giving herself completely, responding without reservation.

From that instant forward, he was tender. Gone was the need to thrust, to bury himself inside her. He hushed her cries with kisses. He moved gently and sank deeply inside her with each succeeding stroke. Nothing could have stopped him at that moment. Their breathing became synchronized, their quiet exclamations simultaneous. And when at last their passion reaching its zenith, the sun seemed to flicker on the horizon and give a final burst of clear, bright sunlight that entered Seth's heart and burned along his veins. Catty called his name, and he pressed one final, beautiful time into her soul.

Hours might have passed thereafter, but as dusk grew around them, Seth was warm and secure and stronger, somehow. The only sound he could hear was Catty's quick breathing. She shifted against him and blew a sigh along his hairline.

She breathed some words into his ear, the same three words that seemed to beat in his heart. But Seth didn't say them aloud. And in a while, he wasn't sure Catty had said them, either. When he raised up on one elbow and looked at her face, stroking a tendril of her hair off her forehead, he saw a smile trembling on her mouth and bright tears glistening in her eyes.

On a painful breath, he began, "Catty, love—"

"Don't say anything." She touched her fingertips to his lips. "Don't spoil it."

He kissed the tears from her closed eyes. "Did I hurt you?"

"You tortured me," she whispered, caressing his face. "By making me wait. Oh, Seth."

He grinned. "'Oh, Seth?' What does that mean?"

She turned a stronger smile up at him. "It means I'm yours for as long as you'll have me. This is wonderful."

Lazily, she writhed against him with unintentional provocativeness. "When can we do it again?"

He laughed. "My dear, as usual, you have the tact of a sumo wrestler. Not for an hour at least, I'm sure. You're all right?"

"A little cold," she admitted.

With a struggle, Seth managed to get the sleeping bag pulled into place. He slipped in beside Catty and zipped it partway. Catty burrowed closer, her small body warm and female.

"Is it always this nice?" she asked, sounding drowsy and content as she snuggled her head on his chest.

"I don't think so," he said, holding her. "I don't remember anything nicer."

"Hmm." She sighed again, her hand straying down his belly to touch him again. "I like this feeling afterward, too." Her fingertips magically caressed him. "Seth?"

"Yes?"

"I—I'm glad it was you," she whispered. "I never knew anyone I wanted to have this with. But now that you—well, I'm glad I waited."

Seth lay silently. He watched the sky as the stars began to shine against the inky blackness of infinity. The earth turned on its axis. Catty's body curled against his and the gentleness of her touch was wonderful, but it was the importance of her words that filled him with desire once again. For a time, he fought the urge. But the lure of Catty's sweetness was too much.

He rolled her onto her back. By starlight, he looked into her eyes.

"I lied," he said, his voice husky with feeling. "It won't take an hour."

She laughed, and the sound was like music—music that could move men's souls.

* * *

In the morning Catty was awakened when a cold, misty rain began to splash her face. The daylight surprised her. For a while, she thought the night might go on forever. Her body ached, but it was a delicious kind of pain. Every muscle felt stiff but satisfied.

She sat up when she realized she was alone.

"Seth?"

He had slipped out of the sleeping bag, and she could see him standing near the edge of the lake in the gray dawn. He had pulled on his jeans, shirt and jacket and was watching the horizon to the south. Catty listened, and in a moment she could also hear the faint drone of an engine.

Their time was over. Catty reached for her clothes, which were piled all over Seth's knapsack.

By the time she was dressed in her trousers and bra, Seth had jogged up to their campsite. Catty looked up at him from the task of dragging on her boots but couldn't speak, couldn't ask the question.

"Yes, it's Kozak," Seth said, when he saw her expression. He tried to be amusing. "Better get dressed, my girl. We don't want Kozak to catch sight of you and crash his plane, do we?"

"Maybe we do," Catty muttered.

There was no pretending this morning, she decided. She couldn't put on a smile.

Seth said nothing until she finished with her boots. Then he extended his hand and helped her stand. She bent quickly to snatch up her shirt, but Seth took her by the shoulders and turned her toward him. He avoided her gaze but helped her into the shirt. When that was done, he commandeered the buttons.

"Look," he said, fastening each one with care. "It wouldn't have worked out, anyway."

"I know," Catty said. "We're too different."

"Or maybe we're too much alike."

Seth finished with the buttons and pulled Catty's sweater over her head. He helped pull her hair through, then played with the strands gently, twisting the curls in his fingers. With a voice gone strangely raspy, he said, "We're just a couple of lonely people, Catty. And we used each other for a little while."

"Yeah," Catty said roughly. "That's it."

He smiled. "Don't use that tone of voice with me, Catty. I know you're lying through your teeth."

Kozak's plane buzzed the island, then began to circle over the lake for a landing.

But Seth didn't turn Catty loose just yet. "I've got something to say."

"Then say it. Your taxi's almost here."

He gripped her tighter and looked steadily into her eyes. He took a deep breath. "Catty, you think you can whip the world single-handedly. And you'll do anything to make sure the rest of us believe you, too. But you're a nice person, Catty Sinclair. You're decent. You've got a heart of gold under that facade you put on."

"I don't need to hear this today."

"You're going to hear it anyway. You're a good woman." Seth bent quickly and kissed her on the mouth. Then, with sudden ferocity, he said, "You deserve better than me."

Catty choked and wrapped her arms around him.

Seth tilted her face up for one last kiss, but when he saw her expression, he cursed softly. "Lips that taste of tears," he said, "are supposed to be the best for kissing. Whoever said that is an idiot."

"Kiss me anyway," Catty said.

He did, but only briefly. His rugged face looked strained, his jaw tense. Then Seth turned away and began to pick up his gear. "Kozak will come back for you later today," he said. "Don't try to find your way back alone, promise?"

"I promise," Catty said.

He turned away. Then, suddenly desperate that he was going to leave then and there, Catty chased him down the hillside. "Seth!"

He turned. "Yes?"

"Will—will I ever know where you are?"

He slung his knapsack over one shoulder and looked at her. Already, there was a distance in his eyes, a coolness in his expression. "I don't know."

"Okay," Catty said. She swallowed. "Goodbye. I hope you fall off the end of the earth. I hope you get shot by some other crazy woman. I hope you get chewed by bears—and—"

"Goodbye, Catty."

He left then, striding off toward the beach and leaving Catty alone. As Kozak's plane touched down on the lake and taxied close to the water's edge, Seth plunged in and waded out until he was hip-deep in the lake. When the plane drew close, he flung his knapsack up over the pontoon and climbed aboard. Catty saw Kozak lean over and shove the passenger door wide open. In less than a minute, Seth disappeared into the plane and Kozak turned it out onto the open water once more. Catty stood still and watched the small plane take off, but she didn't wave. Soon she was alone on the island.

On the plane, Kozak said, "Everything all right?"

"Yeah," Seth said. He leaned toward the window and looked down as the plane lifted and banked over the island.

Catty stood on the ground but didn't look up at the plane. She was too tough for that. She was already walking determinedly back to their campsite. Seeing her there, alone on the island, Seth felt a terrible sense of loss.

"What's the matter?" Kozak asked.

"I don't know," he muttered. "I—I wonder if I'm making the biggest mistake of my life."

That was the extent of conversation for the trip. Kozak politely kept his thoughts to himself until the plane landed near the Canadian shore of Lake Superior.

"I'll go back and get her," Kozak said then. "Right now, if you like."

"Yes, do that. She's probably scared all alone."

"Should I bring her here?" Kozak asked after a pause. "To you?"

Seth shook his head. "No. If my life changes for the better, I'll find her again. And you. You've been a good friend, Mike."

Kozak grinned and shook Seth's hand energetically. But Seth noted a sudden gleam of emotion in his friend's eyes. Sounding choked, Kozak said, "Look me up, if you can."

"Will do," Seth promised. And he meant it.

He struggled ashore to Canada and thought his troubles were over for the time being. He had enough cash to travel, a change of clothes and some food Kozak had brought along.

The only thing he didn't have were the vials.

"Damn her!" Seth shouted when he discovered his loss. "The little bitch stole my formulas!"

Catty didn't wait for Kozak to come back with his plane. She revved up Seth's boat and tried to make her way back to civilization. Unfortunately she got lost.

Fortunately, she was found before nightfall.

But she was found by Joey MacLean and some redneck military man by the name of Pompowsky who was clearly sadomasochistic.

"Young lady," said Pompowsky. "If you are withholding information, I am authorized to incarcerate you in the nearest federal facility for—"

"Oh, put a sock in it," Catty snapped. "You can't arrest me for anything, chum. Go use your guerrilla tactics on someone who will believe that old bluff."

Pompowsky stared at her with rage boiling in his mean little eyes. "Why you little—"

"Listen, you haven't got a couple of dollars to lend me, have you? I need to get to New York as fast as possible."

Pompowsky had no choice but to let her go.

Back in New York, Catty met with the editor of a highly regarded New York newspaper. She had never done business with that particular gentleman before, since her contacts in the newspaper business were of a slightly lower caliber. The editor took her proposal seriously, however.

He eyed her solemnly when she was finished with her presentation. "You realize this amounts to journalistic blackmail?"

"Yes," said Catty, standing at attention in front of his enormous desk. "It's exactly what I set out to do. I want to make sure Seth Barnhurst is safe to come out of hiding."

"And you think telling his story to the world is going to change his situation?"

"People who read this story will agree with me. He was right to steal the formulas. They were created by his father, not the government, and his father wanted them destroyed."

"I'm sure the government will disagree—privately, if not publicly. What if Barnhurst gets killed over this?"

"He won't," Catty said. "Not if you publish this story! By telling everything, we're protecting him. Why, if Seth Barnhurst gets hit by a bus tomorrow, everyone in America will believe the bus was driven by some hired hit man."

"And the public furor over his death would be immense."

"Right. No branch of the government—no matter how secret—could get away with killing Seth."

"What about the formulas?"

"The prototypes have disappeared. They'll never be found."

The grizzled editor looked hard at Catty. "Are you certain?"

Catty lied with a perfectly straight face. "Yes, I'm sure. They've disappeared off the face of the earth."

"And you believe that the American people will take Seth Barnhurst's side in this story?"

"He's a hero," Catty said. "He's a doctor who can't bear the thought of contributing to mass murder. Don't you think everyone will love him for that?"

The editor put on his glasses and studied Catty's article before answering. But at last he looked up at her. "Yes," he said. "I think everyone will love him. And not just because of his actions, Miss Sinclair. Your story is excellent—it comes from the heart. Your passion for this issue is easily apparent. If Seth Barnhurst can come out of hiding, it will be to your credit. I hope he can come out and shake your hand some day."

"Then you'll run the story?"

The editor nodded. "In tomorrow's edition."

"Thank you," Catty breathed.

"Now you can start crossing your fingers," he cautioned.

"Why?"

"Because I can't publish before morning. Seth Barnhurst could die in the next twenty-four hours—and nobody will give a damn."

Eleven

For four days after the story hit the streets, Catty waited for Seth to contact her. But he didn't. No phone call, no letter, no nothing.

At the end of the week, she telephoned Mike Kozak for comfort.

"Maybe he's dead," Kozak said bluntly, clearly annoyed by her call.

"I'm so glad I thought of phoning you," Catty retorted. "You hate my guts, don't you, Kozak?"

"You did a foolish thing, lady. How were you so sure this ploy would work?"

"It's my business," she snapped. "I know a good story when I hear one, and I know how to write it so the public reacts."

"Well, the public reacted, all right. We've still got reporters swarming the lake—and more of them are looking for Seth than Rafer Fernando."

"Oh, people still believe Fernando is there?"

Kozak made a disgusted noise. "Thanks to you, this lake looks like O'Hare Airport. People, planes, helicopters—the works. But most of 'em are looking for Seth, hoping to be the first to actually present him to the public on some kind of silver platter. You did a good job, Sinclair. Seth's name is almost as well known as Fernando's right now."

"Listen, Mike?" Catty gave up trying to sound calm about the situation. "If you hear from Seth, will you—? I mean, have him drop me a line sometime, will you?"

"Yeah," Kozak said. "Sure. If I hear from him."

Catty spent the weekend flying out to see Seth's mother, who lived in an expensive neighborhood north of Los Angeles. But when it came time to hire a taxi to actually deliver her to the house, Catty chickened out. What if his mother hated her on sight? Or worse, what if she believed Seth was dead, too? Catty flew back to New York without contacting anyone.

On Monday, the postman delivered an interesting letter to Catty's box. She opened it immediately. The note was handwritten on cheap notepaper.

Miss Sinclair
Thanks for the publicity. If you want more on the story, meet me behind the Deer Lick Post Office on Wednesday at noon.

Rafer

Catty called an airline reservation number and booked a flight immediately, and wondered that she'd ever doubted Seth's acting ability. He'd even got Rafer's trademark signature down pat on the note.

Naturally, the weather turned bad. Heavy rain and fog kept her flight on the ground too long in New York, and

Chicago was swamped. She took a quick commuter flight into Michigan and—desperate to get to Deer Lick by noon—hired a car and driver to take her the rest of the way. They arrived in a pouring rain—two hours late.

"Look," she snapped at the driver, "I'm just asking you to stick around an hour or so. I may need a lift back to civilization."

"Lady," said the driver, "I've got to get home before sundown myself. So hurry up with your business. You've got fifteen minutes."

"Fifteen—!" Catty seethed, then controlled herself. In the sweetest voice she could muster, she pleaded, "Look friend, I don't want to get stuck in this godforsaken town any longer than you do, so will you please—"

Someone interrupted. "What are you calling godforsaken?"

Catty whirled around in the rain. "Seth!"

He took her by the elbow and leaned down to the driver. "Go home, pal. I'll take her from here."

Catty couldn't breathe. She considered shouting with joy, screaming with frustration, weeping with relief. As it was, she couldn't do any of those things. She let Seth hold her by the arm and just stared. Seth looked just the same as he had nearly a week ago—too-long hair, a scruffy mountain parka over jeans and a flannel shirt. He seemed healthy, and he was certainly handsome. Best of all, he was real. He was alive. Catty felt her heart begin to pound like an entire percussion section.

The hired car drove away, leaving them alone.

"Well, well," said Seth, turning on her. "I hardly recognize you. Did I just hear you use the word 'please?' Have you turned over a new leaf, Miss Sinclair?"

The right words jammed in Catty's throat. "Seth—Seth, it's—I was so scared that you— Damn you, Barnhurst," she shouted, finally getting a grip on her self-control, "where the hell have you been?"

A grin flashed across his face. "Now, that's the Catty Sinclair I remember."

"Stuff the pleasantries! Where have you been, you rat? Why haven't you called me?"

"I've been busy."

"*I've* been busy, buster! You didn't have *five minutes* to pick up a phone and tell me you were safe? I've been worried!"

"Worried? You?"

"I've been *frantic*, as a matter of fact!" Catty tried to keep the level of anger intense, but she couldn't manage. Already, she could feel herself faltering. "I just—I didn't know if—"

"Now, now," said Seth. "Don't fall apart at this stage of the game. I'm all right, love."

At that, Catty burst into tears. She threw her arms around Seth and held him tight. He rocked her gently, murmuring words of reassurance that Catty didn't hear. It was his voice that sounded best—that and the solid heat of his body against her own.

"How about if we get out of the rain?" he said at last. "I've just found where you dumped my boat. What do you say we head up to my place for a chat?"

"A chat? What kind of chat?"

Finally she noticed that he had a steely look in his eyes. Barely controlling the force in his voice, he said, "Surely you can guess what's on my mind, Catty. You have something that belongs to me."

Hastily, she wiped her nose on her sleeve. "Seth, I—"

He gripped her arm hard to silence her. "I want to know one thing immediately, Catty. Do you still have them?"

"Seth, if you'll just—"

He exploded. "Damn you, Catty, I don't know what to expect! For all I know, you've sold them to someone! Now tell me before I wring your neck. Where are they?"

"You—you think I *sold* them?" she sputtered. "*Sold them?* To whom? The martians?"

"Do you have them?"

She sent him a sullen glare. "Yes."

He relaxed visibly. "In that case, I'd like the rest of this conversation to take place when we're completely alone. I don't want any witnesses if I'm moved to strangle you. Shall we?" He gestured toward a boat dock.

With her head held high, Catty preceded Seth to the boat.

They made the trip across the lake in a drizzling rain that Catty found uncomfortable, but surprisingly pleasant. She sat in the bow and kept her eye on Seth during the whole journey, wondering if he was truly angry with her, or if there was still a chance for the two of them. He seemed content to watch her, too, but she couldn't guess what he was thinking. They did not speak.

At last, they reached the cabin. It seemed strange not to be greeted by the dogs, but Catty assumed they were under Kozak's care. Once inside, Seth stripped off his wet parka and set about building a fire and lighting the oil lamps. Catty peeled off her wet jacket and moved to the fire to dry her trousers.

"Now," Seth said at last, facing Catty in the middle of the room. He folded his arms. "How about telling me what you did with my prototypes?"

"They're in a safe place," Catty said primly.

"That's for me to judge," Seth retorted darkly. "Where are they?"

"I've put them somewhere where nobody will tamper with them. So chill out."

"Catty," he said severely, "I explained how dangerous those compounds are. You can't just leave them in your refrigerator or bury them in Aunt Aggie's garden! For crying out loud, they're—"

"The Chase Manhattan Bank."

"What?"

"I rented a safety-deposit box, and it's five floors underground. Even a nuclear attack won't disturb them. They're perfectly safe until you can make arrangements to destroy them."

"You—you put toxic chemicals in a safety-deposit box?"

"What would you have suggested?"

"I'd have suggested that you not steal the vials in the first place! Catty, how could you have done such a stupid thing? Those were my—"

"I know all about them," Catty snapped, facing him boldly. "And I know exactly what you would have done with them, Seth, for the next forty years! You'd have gone on running and hiding—staying one step ahead of—of certain death!"

"Don't be melodramatic."

"Melodramatic? Hey, I talked with one of the guys who was looking for you. His name is Pompowsky, and he's been all over the world hunting down unofficial criminals. He's a bounty hunter, Seth! And he was prepared to kill you to get those formulas. I had to do something."

"So you wrote the story about me."

"Yes," she said angrily. Then, peeking up at him, she asked, "Did you—um—happen to read the story?"

"Yes," he said coolly. "I read it. Not a bad bit of journalism, I suppose."

"You suppose!" Catty blew up. "If you had any idea what I went through to write that piece—"

"All right, it was good," Seth said, holding up one hand to stop her ranting. "It was very good."

"Very good?"

"It was excellent," Seth concluded, his expression softening. "You should be proud of yourself, Catty. You're a first-rate writer."

"Well, I—thank you."

"I should be thanking you." Seth put his hands into the pockets of his jeans. "In fact, I should be thanking you for a great many things, Catty. The first is for saving my neck."

Catty felt herself start to blush. "Well, I didn't—I wasn't really—"

He began to smile. "You wrote a first-rate, hard-news item, and it was picked up all over the world. I read it in Canada, in fact, and after a couple of days of watching the television coverage of the story, I worked up my courage to telephone the lab."

"You mean—where you used to work?"

"Yes. I talked to the man in charge, and they've agreed to let the matter drop—"

"Oh, Seth!"

"Provided I not give any more stories to the press. You included."

Catty's heart was running over with joy. She hugged herself to quell the urge to run into his arms. "I think that's wonderful. I'm so happy for you."

Seth picked up a poker and began to tend the fire in the hearth. He continued to speak as he worked. "The second thing I should be thanking you for is a little less concrete, I guess."

"What do you mean?"

"You and I—we said a lot of things to each other, Catty. Some of them I wish I could take back. But I—well, I want you to know that you were right about me."

"How's that?"

"I'm accustomed to being alone. I tried to handle my problems without any outside assistance. I felt I had to go on protecting the people around me, so I—"

"But we're all on this earth together," Catty said softly.

"Yes." Seth straightened and leaned the poker against the hearth. He turned to Catty then and studied her face. "I'm glad you helped me, Catty. Thank you."

She tried to shrug. "No big deal."

He didn't smile. The only sound in the room was the snap and pop of the fire. In the lamplight, Seth's face looked solemn and vaguely pained.

He cleared his throat. "I wish things had been different for us, Catty. It was the wrong time and the wrong place, I guess."

"No," she said. "Just the wrong time."

He didn't respond. But a flash of hope crossed his eyes, and Catty closed the distance between them. She came to a stop just inches from Seth and began to methodically unbutton her cardigan.

Looking up at him, she said, "We've got more time now."

Seth expelled a pent-up breath. "Catty." As though taking hold of a priceless piece of artwork, he grasped her shoulders and squeezed. "Catty, I think I'm madly in love with you."

She laughed. "Madly?"

"Passionately."

She smiled up at him, her lips trembling. "I'm so glad. Because I'm madly and passionately in love with you, Seth Barnhurst. I thought I'd die not knowing if you were safe."

He hugged her against his frame, burying his hands in her tumbled hair, seeking her lips with his own, holding her as though he was afraid to let her go. Catty kissed him back with all her heart. Happiness bubbled up from inside her, but there were tears, instead of laughter.

"Darling Catty." He kissed the moisture from the corners of her eyes. "Will you stay with me? Help me put my life back together? I need you badly."

"Yes, I'll stay. Hold me."

"All night," he promised. "And for the days and weeks that follow. I don't want to let you out of my sight."

She laughed. "You're going to see a lot more of me in a minute. I'm soaked to the skin. I want out of these wet clothes, please."

His black eyes gleamed in the firelight. "With pleasure."

He finished unbuttoning her cardigan and started on the shirt underneath. Catty reciprocated, hardly able to unfasten the buttons on Seth's shirt for the trembling in her fingers. As they undressed, they gravitated toward the stairs.

"I love you," Catty said when they were finally standing by the bed and nearly naked. "I was never so happy in my life as the moment I opened your message."

"Hmm?" Seth's lips were busy nibbling her throat. "What?"

"Your message. I think I'll save it forever."

Seth straightened, frowning. "What message?"

"The letter you sent. To my apartment."

"My darling Catty," he said patiently, "I never sent a message. I wanted to get back here before I called you. I wanted to get some supplies and—"

"Wait a second. You mean you didn't write to me? Then who did?"

But Seth didn't care. He was stripping off the last of her clothing and filling his hands with her breasts. "Never mind that," he murmured. "I want to make love to you, Catty. I haven't been able to think of anything since I left you."

"But—but, Seth. The letter was signed by Rafer Fernando. I mean, I thought it was *you* pretending to—Seth, are you listening?"

"Umm," was his reply.

Catty sighed. Sometimes there were more important things to do than chase after good stories. She wrapped her arms around Seth and let him press her down among the quilts. In minutes, she forgot all about Rafer Fernando.

*   *   *   *   *

ANOTHER BRIDE FOR A BRANIGAN BROTHER!

Branigan's Touch
by Leslie Davis Guccione

Available in October 1989

You've written in asking for more about the Branigan brothers, so we decided to give you Jody's story—from *his* perspective.

Look for Mr. October—*Branigan's Touch*—a *Man of the Month*, coming from Silhouette Desire.

Following #311 *Bittersweet Harvest*, #353 *Still Waters* and #376 *Something in Common*, *Branigan's Touch* still stands on its own. You'll enjoy the warmth and charm of the Branigan clan—and watch the sparks fly when another Branigan man meets his match with an O'Connor woman!

SD523-1

Silhouette Romance®

AWARD OF EXCELLENCE

LONG, TALL TEXANS

**Diana Palmer brings you the
second Award of Excellence title**

SUTTON'S WAY

In Diana Palmer's bestselling Long, Tall Texans trilogy, you
had a mesmerizing glimpse of Quinn Sutton—a mean, lean
Wyoming wildcat of a man, with a disposition to match.

Now, in September, Quinn's back with a story of his own. Set
in the Wyoming wilderness, he learns a few things about women
from snowbound beauty Amanda Callaway—and a lot more
about love.

He's a Texan at heart . . . who soon has a Wyoming wedding in
mind!

The Award of Excellence is given to one specially selected title
per month. Spend September discovering *Sutton's Way*
#670 . . . only in Silhouette Romance.

You'll flip . . . your pages won't!
Read paperbacks *hands-free* with

Book Mate • I

The perfect "mate" for all your romance paperbacks

Traveling • Vacationing • At Work • In Bed • Studying • Cooking • Eating

Perfect size for all standard paperbacks, this wonderful invention makes reading a pure pleasure! Ingenious design holds paperback books OPEN and FLAT so even wind can't ruffle pages — leaves your hands free to do other things. Reinforced, wipe-clean vinyl-covered holder flexes to let you turn pages without undoing the strap...supports paperbacks so well, they have the strength of hardcovers!

Pages turn WITHOUT opening the strap.

SEE-THROUGH STRAP

Reinforced back stays flat.

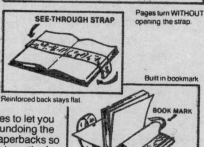

Built in bookmark

BOOK MARK

BACK COVER HOLDING STRIP

10" x 7¼" opened.
Snaps closed for easy carrying, too

COMING SOON...

Indulge a Little
Give a Lot

An irresistible opportunity to pamper
yourself with free* gifts and help a
great cause, Big Brothers/Big Sisters
Programs and Services.

*With proofs-of-purchase plus postage and handling.

Watch for it in October!

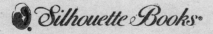

Harlequin Books®

Silhouette Books®